R

Trail from St. Augustine

Also by Lee Gramling:

Riders of the Suwannee

Trail from St. Augustine

A Cracker Western
by
Lee Gramling

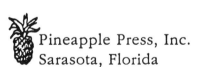

Pineapple Press, Inc.
Sarasota, Florida

Copyright © 1993 by Lee Gramling

Pineapple Press, Inc.
P.O. Drawer 16008
Southside Station
Sarasota, Florida 34239

LIBRARY OF CONGRESS CATALOGING-IN-PUBLICATION DATA
Gramling, Lee, 1942–
    Trail from St. Augustine / by Lee Gramling.
    p. cm.
    "A Cracker western."
    ISBN 1-56164-047-6 (HB) : $14.95. — ISBN 1-56164-042-5 (paper) : $8.95
1. Frontier and pioneer life—Florida—Fiction. 2. Florida—History—English colony. 1783-1784—Fiction. I. Title.
    PS3557.R228T73 1993
    813'.54dc20   93-5214
                               CIP

Design by June Cussen
Printed and bound by Kingsport Press,
    Kingsport, Tennessee

First Edition 10 9 8 7 6 5 4 3 2

For André, who kept the faith

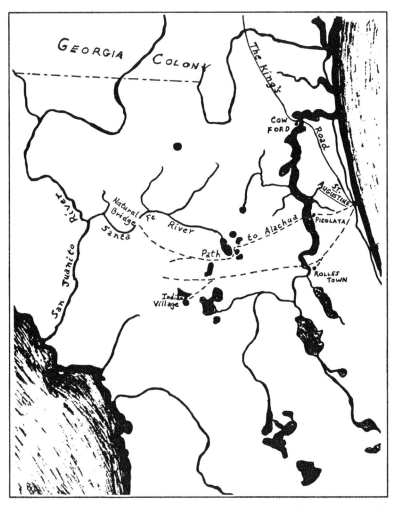

British East Florida, c. 1775

Contents

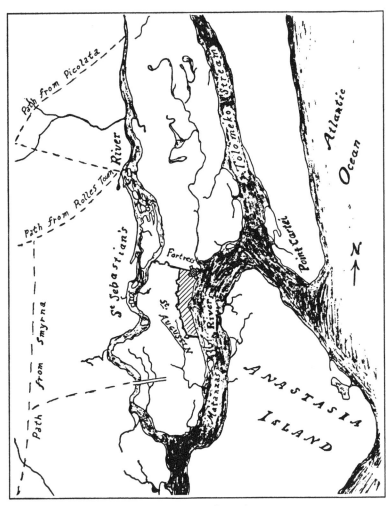

Colonial St. Augustine, c. 1775

1

THE SHADOWS OF THE CYPRESS and live oaks were growing long by the time he reached the riverbank, stretching dark arms over the water to cloak the grassy inlet in purple gloom. Far across the slow-moving current he could see the boatman leaning on the rail of his log raft, smoking a Spanish cigar as he lazily surveyed the mossy treeline on the opposite shore.

He lifted a hand and saw the boatman wave in reply. The burly man stepped up on his raft, dipped a long pole into the water, and pushed off from shore. John Thomas MacKenzie dismounted to check the cinches on the pack mule and his own gray gelding. Then he sat down on the tree-shaded bank to wait.

The raft swung north with the current before turning back toward the western shore where MacKenzie rested. The boatman's powerful arms glistened with sweat in the golden sunlight as he steered his unwieldy craft through the dark waters of the big river.

MacKenzie watched with lazy interest, enjoying the evening coolness and the feeling of new beginnings his return to civilization promised. It had been a good year. His mule's back was piled high with deer and beaver hides that should bring a rich price in the port of St. Augustine.

"Shilling for the crossing," the river man said as he ran the raft to ground at MacKenzie's feet.

"I've no hard money. But there's a-plenty o' pelts. Go ahead and take your pick." The boatman threw a rope around a gnarled tree stump and stepped ashore. He climbed the clay bank to where the mule stood calmly munching leaves from a low bush.

"That you do, neighbor," the boatman agreed. He lifted the blanket that covered the pack and examined the hides, sifting deftly through them with rough fingers. "How 'bout these two deerskins here on top?"

"How about one of them?" John showed his teeth in a good-natured grin.

The river man studied the frontiersman before him,

takng in the lean, well-muscled arms that hung casually at his sides and the powerful legs clad in calf-high deerskin boots. He glanced at the flintlock pistol in the man's belt and the big knife in a fringed scabbard at his hip, not doubting for an instant that his would-be passenger knew well how to use these weapons. Something in the other's steel-gray eyes told him that even without them, this was no man to be taken lightly.

"Fair enough," he replied with an agreeable shrug and a grin.

MacKenzie helped him remove the deerskin from the pack, then gathered the reins to lead his horse and mule onto the raft. The boatman slipped his rope from the tree stump and pushed off from shore.

Neither spoke again for several minutes. The burly man was busy with the current, and his passenger seemed content to stand quietly by, watching the far shore. As the raft entered calmer waters the boatman glanced at MacKenzie. "Been out for long?" he ventured, fending off a sunken tree and turning the craft in sharply toward the landing.

"About a year."

"I reckon that's long enough. With nothin' but snakes and gators and savages for company."

John nodded without replying. His companion fell silent again, busying himself with navigating the grassy shallows near the shore. Before long he was tying up at a wooden pier shaded by two huge live oak trees. A log cabin stood back against the pine woods, a thin column of smoke rising from its clay chimney.

"Supper and bed for another pelt," the river man suggested as John led his animals from the raft.

"Thanks, but I'll be going on to St. Augustine." He placed a foot in the stirrup and mounted, then turned in his saddle. "But if you've some whiskey at hand I might be obliged. It's been long months since I've tasted aught but spring water and bark tea."

The boatman grinned and nodded. He turned and strode to the porch of his cabin, took a clay jug from beneath one of the planks, he returned to where John sat his horse.

"Made it myself," he said as he removed the wooden stopper and handed the jug up. "Not a bad batch if I say so. Help yourself and no charge. If you meet some other travelers on the road, you tell 'em 'bout Robert Ford's whiskey, at Ford's landing. Sell it or trade 'most anything for it. Good for the croup, the gout, quinsy, chills, and snakebite."

MacKenzie took a long pull from the jug, grimacing as the hot liquid burned his throat and warmed his belly. After a moment he took another swallow and handed the jug back.

"As good as any I ever tasted," he said, wiping his mouth with the back of his hand. "You'll have my unqualified recommendation." Then with a casual wave, the frontiersman turned his horse's head to the northeast and cantered off into the shadows lining the white sand trail to St. Augustine.

It was late when he entered the Ancient City. He walked his horse slowly through the balconied streets until he came to a green-painted sign swinging creakily in the offshore breeze. Dismounting at the entrance to the *posada*, he pulled on the bell-cord and a sleepy groom appeared to lead the animals inside.

"Care for them well," John said as he removed a long rifle and bedroll from behind his saddle. "Rub them down and give them both some good corn an' barley." He met the groom's eyes. "And keep the mule's pack in a safe place now. I'll be down to see about it first thing in the mornin'."

Inside, the inn was quiet. Most of the guests had already retired for the night and only one man remained in the common-room, a sailor from his dress. He was curled up on a bench beside the fireplace, evidently sound asleep.

A dark-haired young girl emerged from the scullery, yawning and rubbing her eyes with her fists. John spoke to her quietly in Spanish and she disappeared to return a few minutes later with cold roast meat, bread, and a mug of spiced wine.

"Will you sleep upstairs, *senor?*" she asked as she set the food on one of the long tables. "There is still room for another in the largest of the beds."

"*Gracias, senorita*, but I won't disturb the other gentlemen at this hour. 'Tis a fair night and I'll find a comfortable spot to lay my blankets in the courtyard."

When he had finished his supper and downed the

last of the wine, MacKenzie took out a pipe and filled it from a pouch at his belt. He rose and went to the fireplace, kneeling to pluck out a glowing ember with the iron tongs he found there. As he puffed the pipe to life the man on the bench beside him opened his eyes.

Neither spoke for some time, each studying the other with eyes long accustomed to taking the measure of strangers in the byroads of a hard world. The seaman, whom John suspected had not been sleeping as soundly as had first appeared, raised himself up on an elbow. MacKenzie sat on his heels with the pipe in his hand, regarding his companion through clouds of blue smoke.

He was not a young man, though the effects of sun and wind on the sailor's leathery face made it difficult to guess his actual age. There was a blond stubble on his chin, and thin wisps of sandy hair peeked from beneath a faded stocking cap. His body was small and compact, with the strength and toughness only years at sea could produce. The tendons stood out in ropelike ridges on the backs of his gnarled and powerful hands.

"Evenin'," the older man said at last. He rose to a sitting position with a relaxed fluid motion, crossing his legs beneath him on the bench.

John took the pipe from his mouth. "A good evenin' to you," he said with a slight smile.

"Just in from the back country?" The seaman's pale blue eyes continued their silent appraisal of the frontiersman.

MacKenzie nodded, then replaced the pipe between

14

his lips and drew deeply.

"Been out long?"

"About a year."

The sailor nodded. "Seen a bit of the country, I imagine."

"A bit. I've been trapping and curing hides for trade."

"Never ventured into the wilderness myself, here or elsewhere. Seen lots of blue water, my share of shoals and reefs. Ports and wharves and waterfront taverns from here to Kwangchow. But I've not been beyond the sound of the breakers these thirty years. Allus wondered what it'd be like though, out amongst the forests and fens o' some unknown land, miles from towns and the doin's o' men."

John decided he liked the cut of the weather-beaten man before him. He knew the kind: independent, canny, hard-working — and tough as old rawhide. The sea bred such men and he'd known them in many places, from Providence to Palembang and back again.

"In some ways," he said slowly, drawing on his pipe, "it isn't so different from bein' on the ocean waters, far from land. You're among nature's elements here as there, and you must learn to live with them, not against them."

The older man cocked his head and regarded John closely. "You've been to sea yourself then?" he asked.

"Aye."

"And now you've become a man o' the prairies and the woodlands. Seems a bit of a strange tack that, one course to the other."

"Perhaps." MacKenzie took another deep draught on his pipe. "Perhaps. Yet I do like the wild country. 'Tis simpler in many ways than livin' among towns an' crowds o' men."

"Traveled far in the Florida wilderness, have you?"

"Far enough. From the hills and forests west of us to the great lake and the watery savannas in the distant south. And back through the teemin' bays and fens o' the western coast. It's a land of endless variety, and I have seen much of it."

The seaman fell silent. He seemed to be considering. After a long moment he spoke again:

"You know the back country well, then?" he asked.

"As well as most white men I expect, though that's sayin' little enough."

"Do you reckon you might lay a course to an island on the west coast of the peninsula? A large island at the mouth of a river known as the San Juanito?"

MacKenzie was thoughtful. "I might," he said. "I believe I know the river you refer to, though the natives call it by a different name. But I've never been to its mouth. There are swamps and bogs around that coast for miles in all directions. 'Twould be a much simpler journey by sea."

"Aye." The sailor nodded. "It would, if a man had a ship, and if he cared not that his business be known to one and all." He looked up quickly and glanced about the room. The serving girl had long since returned to her rest and there was no sound or sign that anyone else was stirring in the quiet inn.

The older man looked again at MacKenzie and seemed to reach a decision before continuing:

"You seem a likely lad. The sort a man could count on if the wind should blow up foul of a sudden. It's few who've any knowledge at all o' this Florida back country. Them as does are outlaws mostly, thieves and renegades. You've a different cut about you if I be any judge of men." He paused, then lowered his voice confidentially. "What would you say, lad, to a small business proposition?"

"I'd say," MacKenzie answered calmly, "that it would depend on the nature of the proposition."

"'Tis simple enough," the seaman said with a shrug. "I've a desire to travel to that island I spoke of, and from the landward side. As I've no knowledge o' the wilderness myself, I could hardly venture such a thing on my own. I need a canny woodsman to guide me there and back. And I've a feeling that you might be such a man."

He glanced down at his worn clothing, then met John's eyes again. "From my present state you may well doubt it, but there is the means to make the trip worth your while. You've my word on that. So what do you say, lad? Will y'have a go?"

John sat thoughtfully drawing on his pipe for several minutes. There was clearly more to the man's proposal than met the eye, though what little he had said sounded sincere enough. And there'd been a time when the simple prospect of adventure and unraveling the mystery might have been enough to tempt the reckless spirit which had brought MacKenzie to this land in the first place. But now . . .

He shook his head. "I'll admit you've aroused my curiosity, but my answer is no. When this twelvemonth's labor has been changed to coin of the realm I'll have enough for my present needs, and I have already made other plans." He rose and looked down at the man on the bench. "In different circumstances, perhaps. But for the moment, no."

There was disappointment on the sailor's face, but he did not press the issue.

"Well enough," he said. "'Twas at least worth the askin'." He extended his hand. "I'll be in port a few more days. Call on me when you will, for I'd enjoy hearin' of your adventures in the wilds."

"I'll do that," John said, "and gladly." He took the man's hand. "'Twould please me too, to hear somethin' of your own experiences on the high seas." He crossed to the table and picked up his rifle and pack. Then with a wave to the seaman he stepped out the door and into the walled courtyard adjoining the inn.

Locating a wooden bench beneath a tall magnolia, MacKenzie sat down to finish his pipe. He leaned back, breathing deeply of the salt air and the green smells of growing things. The moon, a quarter full, shone clearly through the leafy canopy overhead.

This courtyard with its trees, grape arbor and thick grass, would be cool even on the hottest of East Florida days. It was completely enclosed, the inn making one side, the stable another, with sturdy wooden walls at the two ends. A bolted gate led to the street, and another to the alley behind the buildings.

It was a peaceful place, John thought, as peaceful and secure as any a man might find in this wild colony. He smiled to himself. Vastly different from some of the places he'd laid his head, not long since.

Yet that realization alone was enough to make him vaguely uneasy, for there was nothing in MacKenzie's experience to suggest security was man's natural state. One who too readily accepted the illusion of security soon grew careless and complacent. And even among civilized men — especially among them, perhaps — this might be the first step to disaster.

Thinking that, it occurred to John how much he had changed since first leaving his father's plantation in South Carolina a lifetime ago, it seemed now. He'd been a boy when he went off to fight in the Cherokee War. By its end two years later he was a seasoned fighting man of nineteen, though still restless and hungry for new adventures.

He'd stayed in the western wilderness for a time, hunting and living off the land, and learning the ways of his former enemies — even living among them for a time. But when he'd seen enough of that country he decided to return home, where there was a place for him as the scion of a well-heeled colonial planter.

The finer points of tobacco and indigo cultivation

held little interest for John however, and the long days of planting and reaping, butchering and preserving and soap making, weighed heavily. The occasional social events were all filled with talk of crops and markets and family affairs, the small things that seem to grow in importance as people become more settled and secure. John did not scorn these things, but he realized that he needed broader horizons in his own life.

His family had seemed as relieved as he was when he signed on as able seaman aboard a merchant ship at Portsmouth "to make his own way in the world." And he had done well, rising to the rank of second mate in the space of only a few years. In the process he'd seen much of Europe, Africa and the Far East.

But his last voyage was aboard a slaver, and the experience had sickened him beyond measure. When they docked at Sunbury to discharge their miserable human cargo, MacKenzie had taken his pay and left the sea without a backward glance. He'd turned his steps southward then, into the wildest frontier in the American colonies.

That was more than a year ago, a productive year and one during which he'd had much time to think about his future. He was getting no younger, and he realized he would not be content to wander forever. So he'd returned to St. Augustine with a plan.

He'd been struck by the numbers of wild cattle roaming free in the wilderness, on lands sparsely populated now that the Spanish had departed with their

Christianized Indians. After selling his hides John would have a stake for breeding stock and supplies, and he meant to start his own *rancho* in the Florida peninsula. It would be a hard task, and a lonely one, but the challenge appealed to him. It was a chance to make his mark on the land, to leave something of John MacKenzie behind in this new country.

His pipe had gone out, and it was late. Untying his bedroll, MacKenzie tossed it onto the soft grass at his feet. Then he took his pistol and laid it where it would be ready to hand. It was a habit he'd followed for years, no matter where he made his bed. He did the same with the broad knife from his belt. Then, wrapping himself in the blankets, he lay on the ground and gazed up at the stars among the rustling leaves overhead. Within minutes he was asleep.

A noise of men shouting brought him instantly awake. The pistol and knife found their way into his hands as if by magic and he rose to step quickly into the darker shadow of a nearby tree. Once there he crouched catlike, listening.

After a short time the cries were repeated, coming from the street some distance to the south. A moment later John heard running footsteps in the alley behind the inn. They stopped at the stable wall.

He crossed quickly to the back of the courtyard and, replacing the pistol in his belt, carefully eased aside the iron bolt that secured the gate. He listened again, but heard nothing. Raising the wooden door slightly so that it would not creak on its hinges, he pulled it back and stepped silently into the alley.

The moon was low and the narrow passage was cloaked in deep shadow. John knew where the running footsteps had stopped however, and he looked in that direction. Seeing a slight movement next to the wall, he drew his pistol and cocked it.

"Stand and show yourself," he said quietly. "And then tell me what all this shouting and running is about that keeps a man from his night's rest!"

The figure did not rise, nor did it move at all from where it crouched beside the stable wall. After a moment John heard the sound of a young woman sobbing.

2

MACKENZIE SWORE UNDER HIS BREATH.
Then he said aloud, "By all that's holy! What is this, now?"

The woman did not answer, but continued to sob quietly, huddled on her hands and knees in the darkness. John lowered his pistol, uncocked it, and replaced it in his belt. He sheathed his knife as well.

"Here, lass," he said gently, "I've no desire to harm a woman." He took a step toward her and reached out a hand, but she drew suddenly back. He halted and lowered his arm.

"Aye," he said after a brief pause, "I don't blame you for being afraid, me coming at you armed and all. But 'twould seem there are others you've cause to fear more. For why else would you be runnin' through dark alleyways and hunkerin' down in the shadows o' the night?"

There was still no reply. The crying gradually ceased and the crouching figure became silent and unmoving. John placed his fists on his hips and cocked his head to one side, watching her.

"Well," he said at last, "it's none of my affair I suppose, one way or the other. Continue your flight if you wish, and I'll vow I never saw you." He turned his back.

"Or if you're of a mind — " MacKenzie indicated the inn-yard " — come inside for a bit till they lose interest in the chase, and we might discuss the matter." There was no response. After a moment he stepped to the opening.

"'Tis your choice," he said, not looking back. "I'll leave the gate open for a short while so you can decide, but then I must close and latch it again for my own peace and security."

He walked into the courtyard and crossed to the opposite side where he had left his bedroll. There he stopped and turned back, leaning against the large magnolia tree with folded arms watching the portal. Soon he saw a slim figure appear in the opening. She hesitated, glanced quickly over her shoulder, then stepped inside and closed the gate. Standing with her back against it, she peered warily into the shadows of the dark enclosure.

When her eyes fell upon John a hand came to her mouth and she started to turn away. Then her back straightened and she seemed to reach a decision. Bolting the gate deliberately, she turned again and began to walk slowly across the courtyard. When she was ten feet from MacKenzie she stopped and regarded him carefully.

She was standing now in a patch of clear moonlight, and he could see that she was about nineteen or twenty years old, with a slim shapely figure and a very pretty face. She wore a simple cotton shift with a wool shawl thrown across her shoulders against the night air. A cascade of auburn hair fell over it to her waist, catching golden highlights from the rays of the moon. Her brown eyes, large now from fear and the exertion of her run, looked directly into his.

John was reminded of a night not long before when a doe had entered the circle of his campfire in a forest of tall pines. It had stood and watched him the same way: poised, wary, unsure whether to run or come closer. Its large dark eyes had held the same mixture of caution and innocence. . . .

Yet it was not the same. For he realized that he felt something far different now, looking into this young woman's eyes, than he'd ever experienced among the creatures of the forest.

"Well, now," he said, managing a smile, "to what do I owe the honor of this nocturnal visit? I'll not deny the pleasure of the meeting, but the circumstances will bear a bit of explaining I think." He kept his voice low, the sound barely spanning the distance between them. The young woman's answer was in the same low tone:

"I had to get away. He . . . he tried . . . to . . ." She paused, watching him, her fist raised to her mouth. Her dark eyes were wide with fear, but there was something else in them too: a smoldering of anger, a flash of fire. John MacKenzie felt suddenly glad that he was not the "he" of whom this young woman was speaking.

"He thought because I am indentured to him that I am his property, body and soul. That I am no more than a slave, to be used for any . . . any purpose whatever!" The words hissed through her teeth and she paused again. Then she shook her head. The bronze hair swirled from side to side in burnished waves.

"I was not raised that way and I'll not live that way! To be poor is one thing. It does not mean that I am . . . a . . ." She fell silent, glaring defiantly at MacKenzie as though he might be no better than that other of his sex.

"Aye," John said quietly, careful to make no move she might misinterpret. "Aye, lass, you speak true enough. This is a new land where all men and women may improve themselves through labor and enterprise. Being poor is but a temporary condition, not a moral state, indenture or no indenture."

He paused, then asked, "Who is he? What might be

the name of this low-born rascal who'd take advantage of a woman alone and in straits?"

"Tyrone!" She spat the word. "James Tyrone. And low-born he may be, but rich enough for all of that. A wealthy planter from the Indies, so he says — though I've had small reason to believe it. Still, he's quite the darling of St. Augustine society."

She shook her head. "I don't believe they truly care for him, but it's few would risk his anger. He has killed six men in duels in as many months. Some say even Acting Governor Moultrie is a little afraid of him."

MacKenzie did not reply. He was trying to remember where he had heard the name of James Tyrone. It was several years ago, and he could not recall the circumstances. But he was certain it was not as a wealthy planter from the Indies.

The young woman had taken a few steps nearer. When she spoke again her voice was cold, with an edge that drew John's eyes to her and made him forget for the moment his attempt at recollection:

"He will not fight another duel soon, I think. For Becky Campbell has put her mark on James Tyrone this night. His right hand will not be fit to hold a sword or pistol for some little time!" Tears came suddenly to her eyes, but she threw back her head defiantly. "Now let them take me! Let him do his worst! I'll kill him, or myself, but I will never, never . . ."

John raised a warning hand and the girl fell silent. An instant later they heard the sound of booted feet outside the courtyard wall and saw the moving glow of lanterns. Men's voices came from the street, just beyond the locked gate:

"Well, gentlemen," a lilting voice said. "I can see that you have managed to find each other with lanterns to light your way. But I do not seem to see that you have found anything else of value." The man spoke quietly, yet with an underlying menace that could be clearly detected in the still night air.

"We've looked in all the streets at this end of the town," a second voice answered. "There's no sign of her. It's as if she's just disappeared entirely!"

"She can't escape," a deeper, rougher voice said. "Come daylight we'll root her out from house to house if need be!"

"William, dear lad," the first man said gently, "I love you for your strong and willing hands when there's dangerous work to be done. I do. Yet I wish sometimes that the good Lord had seen fit in His wisdom to give you half a brain to go with them."

"By morning," the speaker continued, his voice lower still, "tomorrow morning, the girl will have surely spoken to someone. More than one someone, perhaps. Her story will become known. People will talk, as people will do. Now, when they talk, what do you suppose it is that they'll be saying?"

There was a moment of silence. Then the lilting voice, which had dropped almost to a whisper as it asked the question, exploded in rage:

"I'll tell you what they will be saying! They will be saying that Dread Jamie Tyrone, the death of six strong men on the field of honor in as many months, has had the thumb of his right hand bitten through by a sniveling, filthy, half-grown hussy of a backstairs serving wench! They will repeat it with smirks and winks from one end of these Florida colonies to the other! The servants will laugh in the marketplace while the tradesmen split their sides in the ale-houses! The ladies who pass me on the street will smile coyly behind their fans, and their gentlemen will look through me as though I weren't there!

"I will be finished in St. Augustine, gentlemen. Completely. I will be obliged to settle my affairs and slink off in the dark of the night, never to return. My memory will be the joke of these American colonies for a generation to come!

"And that" — the lilting voice became smooth and controlled once more — "my boyos, is why the wench must be taken this night, before even another hour has passed. Now search the streets and the alleyways again, if you please. And do it properly this time! Look for tracks or other signs that will tell where she's been. I promise you that if I must leave St. Augustine in disgrace, I'll be taking no unwanted baggage with me!"

Mackenzie heard two sets of footsteps moving quickly down the street in opposite directions. The third man — Tyrone, he supposed — remained near the inn, pacing restlessly.

John and Becky stayed where they were, unmoving,

listening intently for the slightest sound of the pursuers' progress. It seemed they stood like that for hours, though in reality it could have been no more than a few minutes.

Then they heard the soft crunch of footsteps in the sandy alley behind the inn. The footsteps stopped, moved forward a few paces, then stopped again. The light of the lantern, dimly seen above the far wall, became dimmer still as the man carrying it bent down to examine something on the ground.

Suddenly he swore and began running back the way he had come. In a moment his boots could be heard thudding up the street to where Tyrone waited. A hurried conversation took place, followed by a heavy pounding on the gate to the courtyard of the *posada*.

John motioned Becky behind him into the shadow of the inn's overhanging roof and turned toward the sound. He took out his pistol and pulled back the hammer to check its priming load, then replaced it in his belt and loosened his knife in its scabbard. He approached the gate, and in one swift movement reached forward with his left hand, slid the bolt aside, and stepped back. At the next violent blow the gate flew open, framing two men in its archway.

The one in the foreground was tall, an inch or so above John's own five feet eleven, and slim with a wiry toughness and no-nonsense manner that seemed out of place in the rich satin livery he wore. The image of a hard fighting man was reinforced by knee-high riding boots, a pistol in the sash at the man's waist, and a long ugly scar down his left cheekbone.

When the gate swung open the tall man's eyes showed momentary surprise. Then they narrowed as he measured the frontiersman who stood facing him some ten feet away. He stepped into the courtyard warily and moved to one side so his companion could enter.

The second man was considerably shorter than the first, but with an air of ruthlessness that left no doubt in John's mind as to which was the more dangerous of the two. This man was dressed expensively and in the height of fashion: silk stockings, satin breeches and waistcoat, a long coat of emerald green richly embroidered in gold, and a powdered wig topped by a gold-fringed tricorn hat. His left hand rested on the hilt of a sword that was at once both ornate and businesslike; his right was tightly bound in a linen handkerchief that was beginning to show red where the blood of a fresh wound oozed through.

As the shorter man followed his companion into the courtyard his eyes took in MacKenzie at a glance, then flicked rapidly about the enclosure until they rested on the dark form of the young woman standing in the shadows next to the inn. The corners of his lips curled in a faint smile as he turned once more to John, removing his hat and bowing low from the waist.

"A good morning to you, sir," he said, straightening and meeting the frontiersman's gaze. "I trust the night air finds you in good health."

"Well enough," MacKenzie replied. He spoke calmly, keeping his eyes on both men.

"I must confess to you," Tyrone went on smoothly, "that I find myself in a bit of an embarrassing position at the moment. Earlier this evening it seems I misplaced something that belongs to me. A thing of no great value to be sure, yet still its loss was vexing. I have been at great pains this last hour to recover it."

The Irishman paused, but MacKenzie said nothing. He stood quietly, balanced on both feet with his arms at his sides.

"Imagine my joy upon entering this dark inn-yard," the shorter man continued, "to come at long last upon that which I had lost. You will understand my impatience to return with it to my quarters after this weary night's search." Tyrone's eyes flicked briefly to his liveried companion. "And so I am sure you will pardon me if I do not tarry to exchange pleasantries with a newly arrived visitor to our fair city. Now sir, if you would be so kind as to step to one side . . ."

John made no move. "I think not," he said quietly.

"Sir?" Tyrone's expression suggested that he had not heard correctly. The tall man behind him took a step forward.

"I'm of the impression," John said calmly, "that this young lady has no desire to return to your home this night, nor any other night. I find after discussin' her reasons with her that I am entirely in sympathy with those wishes. So I suggest you leave the premises now, and don't return while she remains here."

Anger flared quickly in Tyrone's blue eyes, but was as quickly brought under control.

"This 'young lady,'" he replied evenly, "as you choose to call her, is no concern of yours. She is a member of my household and is in my considerable debt, having indentured herself for seven years in return for the cost of passage to this new land. I assure you, sir, that the amount was of no small consequence. And I fully intend to have the value of that which I have paid for."

He smiled and spread his hands in a gesture of conciliation. "I've no quarrel with you, sir. I only ask that you stand aside and allow me to recover what is lawfully mine." Tyrone raised his unbandaged hand to his hat, removed it, and bowed low from the waist.

MacKenzie responded in kind, but saw out of the corner of his eye that as he did so the liveried man was edging furtively to one side. An instant later a weighted club appeared in the tall man's hand and he leapt forward.

With catlike suddenness John straightened and grasped the other man's wrist. He brought the arm down hard and twisted, at the same time throwing a left from the waist that almost broke his attacker's jaw. The club fell from the man's grip as John walked in, smashing a right and a left to the body.

A right uppercut with all of John's weight behind it sent the liveried man sprawling, just as a third man entered the courtyard from the street.

The newcomer was so large that his body filled the narrow archway. He wore livery also, but it was too small for his heavy frame and fitted poorly. His face was round and florid, with small narrow eyes set close beside a large nose that had obviously been broken on more than one occasion.

Arriving just in time to see his companion hit the ground, the big man took in the situation at a glance and acted on the instant. Dropping his lantern he launched himself toward the frontiersman with a cry of rage that sounded for all the world to John like the mating call of a bull alligator.

The cry died in his throat as he suddenly discovered himself staring into the dark bore of a cocked and loaded pistol. The large knife was in MacKenzie's left hand, low at his side with the blade up.

"That will do I think," John said with a smile that bared his teeth and showed no trace of humor. "I thank you for the night's entertainment, but the hour is late and I fear I must call a halt to the festivities." With a nod he indicated the tall man who still lay motionless on the grass. "If you'll take up your sleepin' companion now, and depart before there's any serious injury, I'd be obliged."

In the space of a few minutes Tyrone's face had gone from white to red to purple and back to red again. Without thinking he had reached for his sword with his bandaged hand, but the sudden and unexpected pain had helped him overcome the impulse to draw. Now his eyes shone with unbridled fury as he gritted his teeth against the pain and chose his words with difficulty:

"You have me at a disadvantage, sir. That is your good fortune. For were I a whole man not all the saints in Heaven nor all the devils in Hell would prevent me from taking satisfaction for this night's work!" He turned suddenly on his burly companion and struck him a wicked blow across the cheek with his good hand. "Pick up your loutish friend and bear him to his rest!"

With a glance at the pistol, which followed his every move, the big man crossed to his fallen companion. Hefting him easily over his shoulder, he carried him to the gate and out into the street. Tyrone backed to the opening, then bowed once more.

"We will meet again," he said softly as he replaced the gold-fringed tricorn on his head. "Rely upon it. And when we do, sir, look to yourself. For I promise there will be a settling of accounts!" He studied MacKenzie's face for a moment as if memorizing it, then turned on his heel and strode down the street after his servant.

3 ⚜

JOHN FOLLOWED THEM AT A DISTANCE and watched until they were out of sight. Then he returned inside, closing and bolting the gate securely. His back was to the inn when he heard a voice behind him:

"A fair piece of business, lad. A dangerous business, but well managed. Well managed for this night, at least."

MacKenzie turned quickly, his pistol out and swinging in a level arc. His eyes came to rest on a shadowy figure framed in the dark doorway of the inn, a few feet from where Becky stood.

"Easy, lad," the man said gently. "I'm no foe. Wait a bit while I strike a light." He disappeared into the inn and returned with a taper in a tin holder. Its flickering glow revealed the leathery features of the seaman John had spoken with earlier.

As his eyes followed the frontiersman's to the battered pistol in his right hand, the older man shrugged.

"Thought you might need a bit o' help with the bully boys out here. But I reckoned wrong." He uncocked the firearm and replaced it in his waistband. "You've the fighter's way about you lad, no mistakin' that. But still I'm wonderin' if you've any feel for the kind o' vessel you boarded just now."

"I'm grateful for your concern," MacKenzie answered wryly, "but it's never been my custom to rely on others for my fightin'." He uncocked his own pistol and thrust it into his belt, studying the seaman as he did so. After a moment he turned to Becky, who had stood by watching the two men in silence.

"I've forgotten my manners," John said, stepping forward and taking the girl's hand. He led her closer to the doorway. "Miss Becky Campbell," he said with a low bow, "allow me to present myself. John Thomas MacKenzie, late of South Carolina and presently of the colony of East Florida. And this," he turned to the sailor, "is my recent acquaintance, Mr. . . ."

"Robert William Teague the Third," the seaman said

formally, bowing in turn, though a bit awkwardly. "But all the world knows me as Blackpool Bobbie." He spread his lips in a gap-toothed grin. "Blackie, to my friends!"

Dimples appeared in Becky's cheeks as she smiled and curtsied daintily. "My pleasure, sirs. And my heartfelt thanks for your help this night!"

The seaman shrugged. "'Tis little enough help you've had from me," he said, "though you'd be more than welcome to it if needed." He looked from her to MacKenzie, and seemed to be thinking.

"Yet now the fightin's over," he said slowly, "there might be some'at I could offer the both of you by way o' friendly advice. You've a need to chart new courses I'm thinkin', after what has happened here. A word or two from a man what keeps his eyes open and his wits about him might be a help to save you from the shoal waters."

He indicated a rough-hewn table at one end of the courtyard. "Seat yourselves there and take a breath o' the air whilst I have a look around."

John glanced at the girl, then offered his arm and led her to the table. As they sat the seaman pinched out his candle and disappeared inside the inn. He was gone for several minutes, returning at last with a bottle of wine and three mugs, which he set down softly before them.

"All quiet," he said in a low voice, beginning to fill the mugs. "Sound sleepers within. Your little fracas seems to have roused no one but myself." He took a deep draught of wine, wiped his stubbled chin with the back of his hand, then gazed for a long moment at the man and woman across from him.

"You have made a dangerous enemy in this port, friends," he said finally. "A dangerous enemy. 'Tis well known that Jamie Tyrone is no man to trifle with, bad hand or no. He has gold in plenty to buy influence in the colony, and to pay the wages of a lot of hard men besides — men of the sort who'll ask no questions when there's back-street work to be done." He met John's eyes.

"The thuggees you bested tonight were only but a samplin'. Not countin' those and a few others, Tyrone keeps a score of irregular dragoons at his own expense. To help the governor protect the citizens from highway-men and Indian attacks, he says," — the seaman took another swallow of wine — "though there's some as wonders privately who'll protect the citizenry from their protectors now!"

Blackie paused to refill his mug. "But the worst of it," he went on, lowering his voice almost to a whisper, "is that Tyrone is by way of placing the leaders o' this colony neatly in his coat pocket before many more months have passed. The Quality have rich tastes, y' see, and they've not found it easy to live as they would wish in this backward colony. Cash money is always in short supply, and dreams of quick wealth have proved no more than a will o' the wisp.

"Comes Tyrone now, and he is the ready friend of all. His loans are on easy terms, and he's slow to ask for repayment — so long as there's no particular interest by the magistrates in any of his other activities." The sailor shrugged.

"For those few who'd scorn his friendship, there is always the imagined insult, the challenge, and death in the dawn's gray light. Don't let the man's foppish dress fool you. He's a holy terror with both pistol and cold steel!"

Blackie held his mug in both hands and squinted over its rim at his companions.

"In short, friends, James Tyrone is fast becomin' a man who can do what he wants in this colony, with little to fear from the authorities. You can be sure he means to have his revenge on you for this night's work, and he's not the kind to scruple overmuch at the why or the how."

Finishing his wine, the seaman concluded grimly, "There'll be no safe haven at all for you in the Floridas now, I'm thinking — for neither one o' you. Was I you I'd be gone from here before daylight, and seekin' out some faraway port to drop anchor in."

John did not answer immediately. He was frowning deeply. That Tyrone was a dangerous enemy he did not question, though an enemy he had never sought. Yet the hot blood of the highland clans still flowed in MacKenzie's veins. None of his ancestors had been men who took kindly to being pushed. Like them, John felt a sudden dark impulse now to square his shoulders and push back — hard.

He shook his head. "It goes against the grain," he said. "It does. For twelve long months now I've lived in the wilderness, makin' my way with crocodiles, boars, lions and deadly serpents on every hand. To let that little struttin' Irish peacock drive me from it . . ."

"Aye," the seaman said mildly. "Aye, lad. And were it you and him only, or him and one or two others maybe, I'd not be the one to wager against you. But there's more than a score will be on your heels now, and no help to be had from any quarter. It's heavy seas, lad, and a busted rudder. You'd fetch up on the rocks for sure." Blackie paused, then looked from John to Becky.

"And what of this fair lass then?" he asked. "It seems you've made yourself responsible for her, whether that was your design or not. You'll do her no great service with a broken crown and a gullet full of seawater. 'Tis little she can expect from any others, save beatings, slavery and worse. Even putting aside Tyrone's men, there's still the law to contend with, for I heard the man say she was indentured!"

MacKenzie was silent for a time, staring sullenly down at the table before him. Finally he raised his head and glanced at Becky. Then he nodded. "Aye," he said. "Aye, you're right about that, at least. The lass must be gotten to a place o' safety where Tyrone can't lay his hands upon her. And it's little chance she'd have of escape without me, or someone like me, to guide her through the back country."

He drained his wine and set the mug down. "All right," he said. "There's nothing else for it then, and no one else but myself for the doin'. So I'll see you to safety first, lass, and leave the rest be for the time."

Slowly, his fist clenched on the table and he allowed his anger to well up briefly before deliberately putting it aside. "Yet afterward," he said quietly, "I mean to return to this city. I'll let no man tell me where I may or may not live, or what I may or may not do. If Tyrone wants a reckonin' then, he shall have help with the accounting!"

He paused several minutes in thought. Then he turned to Becky.

"A short distance to the north of us," he said, "there's the ruin of an old mission. 'Tis an ancient place, known to few o' the English but easily reached in a few hours' walkin'. I'll take you there tonight and you can remain hidden while I return to the city to dispose o' my hides. I'll sell them to the first ship's captain I meet on the morrow, then rejoin you once more. With steady travelin' we can be in Georgia in a few days, and with luck we'll find friends who'll take you in, beyond the reach o' Tyrone and his gold."

For MacKenzie, to conceive the plan was to put it into action. Without another word he rose and made a reconnaissance along the walls of the courtyard to assure himself none of Tyrone's henchmen were still about. Then he returned to where the others waited and, with a quick parting word to the sailor, took the girl's hand, leading her quickly through the back gate and into the dark alleyway.

They made their way silently through the deserted byways of the sleeping town to a place beside the city wall that John recalled from an earlier visit to St. Augustine. There were few sentries to be concerned about. The mother country was enjoying one of her rare intervals of peace with both the natives and her European neighbors. From what Blackie had told them however, it seemed best that they avoid leaving by the city gates, where they might be detained.

The four-foot mound of earth that surrounded the town was overgrown with cactus planted by the Spanish, and a hedge of Spanish bayonets filled the dry moat beyond. Yet the English had done little to keep up this defensive shrubbery, and in places the plants had died or been trampled by the comings and goings of the colonists. John had made note of one such gap months before, filing it away in his memory against possible future need.

He had picked up a board as they passed one of the many ongoing construction projects in the city, lifting it and carrying it on his shoulder until they reached the low earthwork. Now he laid it flat across the prickly pears on top. After pausing to listen and look carefully in all directions, he took the girl's hand and led her quickly over the barrier into the ditch beyond.

Removing the board and hiding it where it would be ready for his return, MacKenzie guided Becky carefully through the hedge of needle-sharp spines. Once past it, they climbed the shallow bank and struck out to the north and west between rows of cultivated fields.

After a few minutes they came to a second earthwork, running east to west across the narrow peninsula that contained the ancient city. This wall was undefended and easily crossed. Yet John explained in a hurried whisper that silence and stealth were still necessary. For on the other side, only a hundred yards away under the guns of the Fortress St. Marks, lay the cabins and huts of a sizable Indian village.

Skirting this settlement to the west, they soon came to a path leading northward along the San Sebastian Inlet. After putting perhaps a mile of this route behind them John slowed their pace, continuing on for several more miles before turning off onto a much fainter trail which wound in among the trees and palmetto brakes of a small wooded hillock. At last they halted in a clearing surrounded by a thick stand of pine and cedar.

The ancient mission had been constructed of wood, and little remained of it after years of abandonment to the lush foliage and frequent rains of the Florida climate. There was part of a clay chimney still standing, and next to it a jumble of brush and logs where a wall had collapsed, forming a rough lean-to.

After inspecting this shelter to be certain it was free of snakes and other wild creatures, John led Becky inside on hands and knees. He squatted beside her in the darkness.

"It is a cheerless place," he admitted, "and perhaps a bit of a fearful one at this hour o' the night. But you'll be safe enough I think, for few men know that it is here. And most wild beasts this close to the settlements will keep their distance when they catch the human scent. In any case, I should be returnin' before many hours have passed."

Becky smoothed her skirt about her on the ground and shrugged. "It is not so likely I'd fear the lesser vermin," she said boldly, "after a fortnight in Tyrone's household!" She turned her head toward him in the dim light. "Do not you worry. I will make do." A moment later John felt a hand brush his cheek. "And thank you," she added quietly.

With a quick farewell, MacKenzie left the shelter and stepped out into the clearing. In an instant he had merged with the shadows of the night, making his way quickly back to St. Augustine in the long, distance-eating strides of the woodsman.

The eastern sky glowed fiery orange as the huge ball of the sun peeked above the trees of Anastasia Island, its clear light turning the gentle waves of Matanzas Inlet into dancing points of gold and silver. John breathed deeply of the soft morning air as he strode to the waterfront, leading his pack mule.

Even at this early hour there was much activity among the ships and lighters moored in the harbor. Sailors were washing down decks and scraping barnacles from wooden hulls, cargoes were being hastily loaded and unloaded, and stern-faced captains and mates were noisily overseeing these activities through clouds of steam from mugs filled with tea, coffee, or stronger concoctions.

As he neared the wharf MacKenzie studied the closest of these officers, a large man with bloodshot eyes whose gruff shouts and curses clearly testified to his determination to be off on the morning tide, despite the apparent ravages of a night's carousing on himself and his crew. Rather than judge the man by these outward appearances however, John turned his eyes to the two-masted schooner which lay at anchor close by. It was trim, shipshape and spotlessly kept up, and was a far better indicator of the captain's seamanship than the temporary color of his eyes. Looping the mule's lead rope around a nearby piling, MacKenzie approached the big man.

"A good day to you," he ventured, smiling. "Where might you be bound for this fine morning?"

"New York, by way o' Charleston and Portsmouth," the other replied, "if these slug-a-beds can get the lead out of their breeches in time to catch the tide 'cross the bar! —You there!" he shouted to a man at the forward hatch. "Secure the corner of that canvas, or by the Almighty I'll see you lashed below with a spoon for a bail at the first sign of heavy weather! Smartly, now!"

MacKenzie watched the sailor jump to his task, then spoke again: "D'you suppose," he asked, "you might have a wee bit o' room left for another small cargo? I've some fine furs here, well scraped and preserved. And I've a desire to return to the back country without undue delay. I'd be willin' to consider any price you might think is fair."

The captain took a swallow of coffee and glanced at the pack mule, then regarded John through narrowed eyes. He hesitated a long moment before replying.

"It's tempted I might be," he said at last, speaking quietly and deliberately. "For good furs do bring a fine price these days on the New York wharves." He hesitated again, and finally shook his head. "But no, lad, I dare not chance it. The risk is too great. For me and, I'll venture to say, for every other ship's captain in St. Augustine!"

At John's look the man lowered his voice even more. "There's word been carried just this hour past, lad, to every master in the harbor. 'Tis said there's a frontiersman with pelts to sell who has an enemy in high places, close to the governor himself . . " The captain paused and his eyes swept the shore beneath heavy brows.

"'Twas suggested," he continued softly, "that to do business with this man might bring charges o' trading in contraband. But worse than that, 'twas said that all the harbor pilots in St. Augustine have been warned off from any ship that has dealin's with him, now or in the future. D'you know what that means, lad?" He nodded toward the distant breakers at the mouth of the inlet. "That is the most dangerous channel in the Americas out there. Not one of us could be sure o' reaching the open water without a pilot to guide us through its constantly changin' shoals and shallows, — t' say nothin' of any future landfalls here!" He met John's eyes.

"Now, I won't say you're the frontiersman in question, and I won't say that you aren't. But you're clearly from the back country, and you have furs to sell. You see how it is." The captain took another sip of coffee and started to turn away. "I'd be obliged if you'd be getting along now," he said over his shoulder. "Even to be seen talkin' with such a man as you could have its dangers. I'm sorry, lad, but I'm afraid there'll be no market for your goods in St. Augustine this day."

John frowned and nodded slowly. "Aye, so that's the way of it, is it?" He glanced up and down the quay, moving only his eyes. A rough-looking man had appeared, leaning against a palm tree some fifty feet away. He was staring in their direction.

The man's face was not familiar, but the satin livery he wore was of a style MacKenzie had seen not many hours before.

"I'll trouble you no further," John said quietly, "but it's grateful I am for your honest talk." He stepped back and untied his mule's lead rope, coiling it in his left hand. "Perhaps another time."

Without looking again at the liveried man, MacKenzie started north along the waterfront, leading the pack animal. He walked slowly and deliberately, turning his head neither to the right nor to the left. When he was almost at the glacis below the towering gray walls of the Fortress St. Marks, he heard the hoofbeats of many horses.

4

JOHN HALTED AND TURNED SLOWLY, his
right hand hovering an inch from the butt of his pistol.
A half dozen riders were approaching on the road in front
of the fort, and that many more from a side street nearby.
He had kept the mule on his landward side as he walked,
so that now he stood looking over the pack as the men
drew rein in a semicircle around him.

The leader, a large man with two pistols in polished

black saddle holsters and a saber at his hip, rose in the stirrups and looked down at MacKenzie. He touched the brim of his tricorn with a forefinger and spoke with elaborate courtesy:

"A good morning to you, sir. It is a fine day for a stroll on the quay, though a bit early for a landsman to be abroad. Who might I have the honor of addressing?"

"Who is it then," MacKenzie replied softly, "that wishes to know my name?"

"Bonneville Richards," the large man said, a hint of hardness creeping into his voice, "at your service." He bowed slightly. "Captain of the St. Augustine Light Horse, charged with keeping the peace in this city and its environs. We have had reports of a troublemaker, a renegade from the back country who flouts the law and attacks our citizens without provocation." His eyes held MacKenzie's. "You seem to fit the description."

"Do I?" John's tone was mild. "I have never been one to seek trouble with those who wish none with me, for I'm a peaceful man. Perhaps your description was of someone else."

"Perhaps." Richards smiled without humor. "In that event I am sure the matter will be resolved soon enough. But in the meantime I'm afraid I must oblige you to come with us."

MacKenzie glanced at the riders around him. All were tough, hard men, but they wore no uniforms. Nor were their weapons and harness of standard British issue.

"The St. Augustine Light Horse," he said thoughtfully. "I'd not heard of such a company before, and I've been in the colony for some time. Are you recently arrived from the islands perhaps, or are you local militia?" He looked up at the large man. "Or could it be that you do not represent the Crown at all, but some private citizen?"

"That is none of your affair," Richards replied curtly. "We are twelve, you are one, and we have our orders." He glanced at the men around him. "Take him" he said, and drew his saber.

As the troopers began to dismount, MacKenzie acted. His left hand dropped from where it had rested on the mule's crupper and he grasped the animal's tail, giving it a sharp and painful twist. As the mule began to bray and kick, John stepped quickly to the water's edge, turned, and dove into the sound.

The cavalry horses, likely to be steady enough in the face of shot and steel, wanted no part of an enraged mule. They backed and reared furiously, throwing several of Richards' men to the ground. It was a few minutes before the others could regain control of their steeds, dismount, and reach the bank. By then John was a good fifty yards away, swimming strongly.

He glanced back in time to see pistols leveled at him, and dove suddenly beneath the surface. Balls spattered the water above his head, but lacked the force to penetrate the depths where he now swam. None of the dragoons had been armed with muskets.

Regaining the surface and taking in deep gulps of

air, he saw the troops hurriedly reloading while Richards galloped toward the gates of the fortress on John's left. To his right Anastasia Island lay half a mile away across the open water of the inlet. From there he would have to wait for night and swim the ocean channel, or else escape southward, in a direction opposite to where Becky awaited him. Ahead was the Tolomeko River, his best route under the circumstances but one that would take him directly under the walls of the fort.

John made his decision instantly, striking out northward and hoping to put as much distance as possible between himself and the fort before the garrison could be roused. He knew he could easily be seen from the high coquina walls, and musket fire from above would find less resistance from the water, even if he could manage to remain under until he was beyond their range — which he knew he could not do.

A moment later Richards reached the outer bastion of the fort and stood in his stirrups to call for the lieutenant of the watch. "Alert the garrison!" he shouted roughly. "A prisoner's escaped, swimming the sound! Send some men to the walls and you can shoot him down like the dog he is!"

It was several minutes before an officer appeared on the drawbridge. He approached with a slow unhurried tread, stopping a few feet away from the rider. Removing his hat, the young man bowed formally.

"My compliments, Captain. What seems to be the difficulty?"

"An escaped prisoner, a *bandito* from the back country! He's swimming the sound, beneath your very walls! Call out your men!"

The lieutenant looked up into Richards' florid face. "With pleasure, sir. If you will show me your warrant . . . "

"Warrant! There's been no time for warrants! The man's only just escaped!"

"No warrant?" A puzzled frown darkened the young man's handsome features. "That is most irregular. I am not sure whether I have the authority . . ." He hesitated, seemingly in deep thought. "Perhaps I should call the major. But he was celebrating rather late last evening, you know, and he's dashedly irritable if wakened before his usual time." The lieutenant shrugged and smiled up at the captain. "It really would be less awkward if you could provide me with a proper warrant."

Richards glared down at the young man's blandly smiling face, then with a sharp curse he wheeled his mount and galloped back to organize his own troops for the pursuit. Damn that lieutenant for a petty, sanctimonious, muddle-headed fool!

Lieutenant Trevor's smile broadened slightly as he strode back across the drawbridge into the fort. Tyrone had made a minor tactical error in not securing a warrant from the magistrate before setting his dogs on this frontiersman, whoever he was. But he had made a far larger one when he'd killed Trevor's best friend in a thinly provoked duel two months earlier.

❖   ❖   ❖

MacKenzie lay among the tall reeds that bordered the Tolomeko River, catching his breath and watching for any sign of pursuit. That there would be a pursuit he had no doubt.

The fort was a mile behind him, hidden from view by islands of trees and brush that dotted the marshy grasslands. Why there had been no firing from the high walls he had no idea, but he was not one to question Dame Fortune's bounty. He had escaped capture for the time being at least, and he gave no serious thought to the why or the how of it.

What he was thinking about was the course he must take from here. He had only the sodden clothes on his back and his knife. He'd managed to keep his pistol with him, but it was soaked and useless. His rifle was still at the inn with his horse and the rest of his outfit, including spare powder and ball. He was clearly in poor shape for a fight, even if the number of his foes had been fewer. That must be avoided then, for the time being.

He'd lost his stock of furs, representing a year's hard work and his stake for the future. There seemed little hope of getting them back, given Tyrone's influence in the colony and John's own lack of connections. The Irishman had managed to make himself more than a passing annoyance now. The matter had become an intensely personal one, and MacKenzie swore softly as he promised himself that there would indeed be a reckoning, soon or late.

He returned his thoughts to his present situation. All

around him lay low salt marshes, covered by grass and water, and little else except where occasional clumps of trees and brush marked a small hammock of slightly higher ground. There was little cover to hide him from the eyes of his pursuers, which even now might be scanning the barren flats from some point inland.

He must find a way to higher ground and better concealment. Then he could return to the abandoned mission where Becky waited and give some thought to their next move. There was a chance he might recover his horse and outfit if he could enter the city after dark and escape again without being detected.

The closest hammock was three hundred yards away, densely overgrown with scrub oak and palmettos. It offered concealment if he could reach it unseen, and dryer land where he might rest and air his wet clothing. If he climbed one of the taller trees he would have a good view of his surroundings. There were a few other islands beyond that one, and a mile away the dark treeline of the forest beckoned.

His eyes moved slowly over the green and white expanse, carefully noting every subtle variation in color. After a moment he thought he could see a deeper shading, winding through the grass to within a few yards of the hammock. He looked more carefully, and could make out the thin white line that marked the sandy bank of a shallow creek. It seemed to enter the river about a hundred yards north of where he now lay.

Moving slowly, taking care to disturb the reeds

around him as little as possible, he began to inch his way along the riverbank. In a half hour he had reached the mouth of the creek. It was about three feet deep, with low banks that would provide concealment as long as he remained in the water.

On his hands and knees, half crawling, half swimming, John made his way upstream to a point opposite the hammock. He took his time, moving with care to avoid splashing. Though he paused often to listen, he heard nothing that would indicate any of his pursuers were nearby.

Raising himself cautiously so that his eyes were barely above the sandy bank, he carefully scanned the shadowed recesses of the hammock. Then he let his gaze roam over the grassy flats. A sand crane was making a slow lazy passage to the distant trees, and somewhere a mockingbird complained loudly. Crickets buzzed nearby. There was no other movement or sound in the steaming salt marsh, already sweltering in the midmorning sun.

The hammock was less than twenty feet away. After taking several minutes to study his route, John eased himself over the bank and started forward on his belly, hugging the ground and pulling himself along with his elbows. When he reached the higher ground he continued crawling until he was well within its hidden recesses.

Among the thick undergrowth it was green and cool. John paused again to listen, then began removing his sodden clothing. His jacket, shirt and stockings were hung on nearby limbs to dry. His boots he stuffed with Spanish moss to absorb the moisture, then set them in a patch of sunlight on the sandy ground. Barefoot, he squatted in a small clearing and gazed up at the trees over his head.

A large sweet gum a few yards away seemed to offer a good vantage point from which to view his surroundings, and the climbing would not be difficult. After studying it briefly, he rose and crossed to its base, then started upward. When he could see across the salt flats in three directions he looped his leg around a branch and scanned the horizon carefully.

To his right was the river, and on its other side the green and white mass of high sand dunes. Beyond these lay the Atlantic Ocean, its deep blue visible in places between the dunes. Ahead of him the open expanse of salt marsh was broken only by meandering streams and occasional distant hammocks. On his left he could see the darker green of the forest, some three-quarters of a mile away. Closer in that direction and slightly behind him was another hammock.

The swampy ground around John's refuge would not encourage men on horseback to cross it to make a detailed search. There was too much chance of quicksand or hidden sinks that could lame an animal. The problem from his point of view was that there was also little cover to aid him in his escape.

As he turned his head to examine the hammock on his left more carefully, John saw the remains of an old

Spanish causeway leading to it from the mainland. A shallow ditch ran along both sides of the causeway. If he could reach that ditch . . .

Suddenly a movement caught his eye. A rider had appeared on the causeway!

MacKenzie held perfectly still, knowing that movement attracts the eye more quickly than an unusual shape or color. He was partly concealed behind leaves and Spanish moss, but since he could see the horseman he realized that the man could, if he knew where to look, see him as well.

The rider's clothing left no doubt in John's mind as to his loyalties, nor to his purpose in being there. He was dressed in the conspicuous satin livery of Tyrone's servants. As the horse crossed the causeway at a slow walk, MacKenzie thought he recognized the mounted man himself. He was reasonably sure it was the tall fellow he had fought in the inn-yard the night before.

Upon reaching the end of the causeway the liveried man dismounted and led his horse among the trees. As he disappeared from sight John eased his body around the trunk of the sweet gum to a position from which he could watch without being himself so clearly exposed to view. Then he waited to see what the other would do.

A moment later the man reappeared on the side of the hammock nearest MacKenzie. He stood for a long time, examining the salt flats carefully. His eyes lingered on the woods where John watched, but after a time he looked away, apparently satisfied to have seen nothing out of the ordinary.

Soon he withdrew again among the trees, coming into view a few minutes later at the end of the causeway. He turned toward the mainland and raised a hand in a beckoning signal. Shortly afterward three more riders appeared. They crossed the causeway to the hammock and dismounted. One of them, John noted with interest, seemed to be an Indian.

These latest arrivals appeared to have come prepared for a lengthy stay. There were blanket rolls behind their saddles, and sacks of other supplies which they removed and carried into the woods upon dismounting. Their horses were led among the trees, and a few minutes later smoke from a campfire began to filter through the leaves over the adjacent hammock.

"Watchers," John told himself. "Pickets to keep an eye on the marshes for the unwary fugitive." No doubt there would be others, at different locations in the forests and savannas surrounding the city. Tyrone was taking no chances. His zeal in the matter was flattering — if a trifle annoying.

When he'd satisfied himself that at least three of the men on the neighboring hammock intended to remain there, John waited his chance, then descended to the ground as their attention was temporarily distracted by food and hot tea. Kneeling in the clearing where his clothes aired, he considered the situation.

It was not yet noon, and under the circumstances

his best opportunity for escape now lay after dark. The chances in daylight with three watchers so close by were slim at best.

The old mission where he had left Becky was off the traveled routes, and its location was not well known among the recent British arrivals. The girl should be safe enough there if she did not become restless and start to move about. Would she remain, even though John would be almost a day late in returning? He hoped so, and he thought it likely. She seemed a steady sort of a girl, not given to panic or unconsidered action. Besides that, she had nowhere else to go.

There was nothing more John could do at the moment. He wanted dry clothes, and he needed rest — he'd gotten little enough of the latter the night before. He might as well get some sleep while the heat of the day took care of his clothing.

Carefully drying his knife with Spanish moss, Mac-Kenzie also wiped the scabbard and hung it on a limb nearby. Then he climbed to a low thick branch that overhung the clearing and situated himself as comfortably as possible in the angle between the branch and the trunk. Placing the knife's hilt beneath his right hand, he closed his eyes. He would sleep lightly, as he always did in the wilderness, and trust to Providence that he would awaken quickly if danger threatened.

A slight breeze stirred the leaves overhead. The mockingbird was still complaining, and a cricket chirruped softly. In minutes John was asleep.

5 ⚡

W HEN HE WOKE, the shadows were already growing dark within his forest hideaway. The cricket, or its cousin, was still buzzing, and a bird was scratching for its supper in the brush nearby. John lay still for several minutes, but he heard no other sounds.

He descended the tree and dressed quickly, donning all but his jacket. His clothes were not completely dry, but they would have to do. He replaced the knife in its scabbard and shoved it behind his belt, then picked up the pistol. It was dry now, but would need greasing to prevent its rusting quickly from exposure to the salt water. He had no grease. That task, like some others he'd set for himself, would have to wait.

Placing the pistol in his belt, he crossed to the sweet gum tree and began to climb, working his way up slowly and keeping the trunk between himself and the neighboring hammock. A thin streamer of smoke hung in the reddening sky, evidence enough that Tyrone's men were still present. John found a comfortable perch in the crotch of a limb and studied the wooded island across from him.

In a few minutes one of the pickets appeared between two trees at the edge of the salt marsh. He scanned the grassy landscape for a short while, then withdrew to reappear at a different spot where he repeated the performance. MacKenzie waited patiently while the man made a complete circuit of the hammock. It seemed only one picket at a time was keeping watch. Assuming the others were still there — and that was the safest assumption — they would be likely to remain by the campfire until it was their turn on duty.

The sun was low on the horizon, but it was still about two hours till dark. Time enough. Descending the tree carefully, John took up his jacket and, using the buckskin fringes, some of which he removed with his knife, tied it so that it would make a secure sack. Then, with the knowledge and patience of years in the wilderness, he began to search the nearby palmetto thickets. He had a plan.

Escape was the most important thing of course. He must waste no time in rejoining Becky, putting together some sort of outfit, and getting the girl safely out of the country. But being hunted like a common thief was a new experience for John, and not one he enjoyed. It made him angry. And he had decided to give his pursuers something to remember him by before finally taking leave of them.

An hour later he returned to the sweet gum and laid his sack, its opening securely tied, on the ground beside it. Then he climbed to his former perch and settled himself for a patient wait. He wanted to study his "watchers" at length, to be sure of their numbers and routine. For what he had in mind it would not do to assume something he could determine through observation, nor to trust to chance when there was no need.

Carefully, so as not to shake the branches around him, John plucked some leaves and placed them in his mouth. He would prefer a pipe, but could hardly spare the time or the risk involved in striking a fire under the circumstances. The sweet leaves would be an acceptable substitute.

When the stars had appeared in the evening sky, he climbed carefully to the ground. He was now satisfied that there were three, and only three, men on the neighboring hammock. He'd seen nothing of the tall man who had brought the others there, and probably that one had left on different tasks some time ago. The three who remained were taking turns on watch, as he had surmised earlier.

The glow in the western sky soon faded completely. John picked up his sack and stepped to the edge of the woods. He looked across the grass at the spot where his would-be captors waited. He knew the trees at his back would prevent him from being silhouetted against the night sky, and, though the moon was already up, its light would be more of a help than a danger as long as he avoided skylining himself and moved cautiously.

Cautious movement in the wilderness, silent and stealthy as an Indian, had long been second nature to John MacKenzie.

He could see the glow of a large campfire among the trees on the hammock across from him. It had been built up with pine needles and fat knots as darkness fell, not, John was sure, by the Indian he thought he'd identified among the watchers. Such fires were made by white men for warmth and companionship, to make the darkness seem farther away. They helped a man used to cities and people feel less alone in the wilderness. Beyond that they were worse than useless.

In fact there were serious disadvantages to a big fire, as the natives well knew. Besides consuming large quantities of dry wood, which took time and effort to gather, a bright fire made it easier for an enemy to locate your camp at night, and harder for you to see him approaching it. Night blindness from staring into such a blaze could easily be the last mistake a tenderfoot ever made.

That fire would be a help for what John planned. There was a good chance that at least one of the pickets would be blinded and useless if suddenly forced away from the campfire — perhaps two of them, if the Indian was the one on watch.

He waited until the picket across the way appeared, silhouetted clearly in the glow from the campfire. When the man left his vantage point to continue his rounds, John began counting slowly to himself. His earlier observations had given him a good idea of how long it would take the guard to reach the opposite side of the hammock.

At last, like a darting shadow, he moved.

Keeping low to the ground, MacKenzie crossed the marshland to the neighboring hammock quickly and silently, entering the trees at some distance from the campfire. Kneeling in a clump of palmetto, he listened for several minutes to the night sounds and the low voices of the men beside the fire. He could not make out what was being said, but the sound at least gave him a definite location for two of his enemies.

When he had caught his breath, he moved again, taking his time and treading lightly as he circled around the clearing where the two men talked beside the fire. He kept a wary eye out for the third, but saw nothing of him. Probably he was still on the far side of the hammock.

Suddenly John stopped, unmoving and scarcely

breathing. The men's mounts were tethered not ten yards from his present position. His route had placed him downwind of the animals, but he knew the slightest sound might excite them to a noise that would bring Tyrone's men to investigate.

He approached the three horses cautiously. They eyed him with suspicion and their ears went up, but John kept his manner relaxed and confident, and at last he drew near enough to place a hand on the neck of the closest one, a big bay. He spoke softly in its ear and calmed it, then carefully proceeded to do the same with the others.

Using his knife, he quickly fashioned halters and lead ropes from the picket lines and led the animals a short distance away toward the causeway to the mainland. Bunching the ropes, he tied them to a nearby scrub pine with a slip knot. Then he returned on cat feet to crouch with his buckskin sack a few yards from the campfire.

The two in the clearing were big, tough-looking men, of the sort John had seen often on the waterfronts of the world. They were dangerous enough in their own element no doubt, but they were clearly not woodsmen. The Indian, if such he was, was nowhere in sight.

MacKenzie made a mental note of caution to himself. He believed he could handle the two men before him if need be, though in the forest he saw little danger of being cornered by them. A native, with the fighting skill and knowledge of the wild country typical of his race, might be a different proposition entirely.

With infinite patience John eased himself closer to the fire, using as cover the lush undergrowth that surrounded him on every side. When he was six feet away and could feel the warmth of the hot blaze, he halted in the shadows and untied the sack he'd made of his buckskin jacket.

Loosening the folds with care, he grasped the writhing object inside in a grip of iron. Then, seeing that both men's eyes were turned toward the fire, he rose suddenly and flung the large serpent into the clearing between them.

The diamondback lit and coiled like black and gold lightning. For a brief instant there was silence, broken only by the furious staccato *brrrrr!* of its rattles. Then this sound was lost in the terrified cries of the men and the crash of heavy bodies charging into the brush away from the clearing.

MacKenzie heard these sounds from a distance, for he was already moving swiftly toward the horses when the snake hit the ground.

Reaching the spot where he had tethered the animals, John released the slip knot with a quick pull. In a single fluid motion he gathered the ends of his rope halter and swung up onto the big bay, mounted bareback. The men's saddles and harness lay on the ground nearby, but there was no time to collect them.

As he turned to shift the lead ropes of the other two horses to his left hand he saw a dim movement among the palmetto fronds of a brake a few feet away. An instant later a figure emerged from the trees, crossing the small clearing toward John in a crouching run.

The Indian closed the distance between them quickly. With a final rush and a leap he was on the back of the bay, behind MacKenzie. The naked knife in his hand gleamed in the moonlight as he raised it to strike.

John responded instantly, dropping the ropes and turning to seize the red man's wrist in his left hand. At the same time he brought his right forearm up hard, smashing a painful blow to the Adam's apple. He followed through, lifting his forearm higher while his left hand twisted and jerked the knife arm down sharply. A leg hooked behind the Indian's knee and a sudden turn of his body sent his opponent tumbling to the ground.

MacKenzie heard the thud and the sharp grunt as the other man landed, but he wasted no time watching him fall. Grabbing a handful of mane he kicked and slapped the big horse on the rump, and in a second they were away. John was lying flat and hugging the big horse's neck as it leapt among the trees beneath low-hanging limbs.

A minute later they were into the open, galloping full out across the moonlit causeway. John took a firmer grip in the thick mane with his left hand and leaned forward, struggling to reach the loose halter rope that bounced wildly beyond his outstretched fingers.

When the animal came to the end of the causeway it slowed to climb a grassy bluff and MacKenzie got his hand on the rope at last. Grasping it firmly, he sat up and began to bring his charging mount under control. By the time they had reached the distant treeline he had managed to halt the bay and take a look behind him.

The other two horses had followed them at first, but had turned aside upon reaching the mainland. John saw them now, entering the woods a hundred yards away. He had no time to waste trying to catch them, but at least the animals' escape would delay pursuit temporarily.

A moment later he saw three human figures emerge from the shadowy hammock onto the causeway. They were looking in his direction, but had not yet seen him against the dark background of the forest.

Giving in to a sudden reckless impulse, MacKenzie raised a hand and let out a wild whoop of challenge and triumph. As Tyrone's startled men swung their bodies toward the sound, he turned the bay's head into the forest and cantered off among the tall pines.

It took less than an hour to reach the hidden trail to the ruined mission, where John hoped Becky was still waiting for him. He dismounted and walked the remaining distance, advancing warily. His senses were alert for any sign of pursuit, or of unwanted visitors concealed in the shadows ahead.

There were none however, and as he entered the clearing he breathed a sigh of relief when he saw the girl's slim figure emerge from the rough shelter where he had left her the night before.

Becky waited until he drew near. Then she spoke quietly, but with more than a hint of impatience. "It's you, is it? I was beginning to wonder if you'd decided to leave me to the beasts of the forest while you spent your profits on the pleasures of the town. It's no food I've had this long day past, and . . ."

When she saw the expression on his face her voice changed. "Is it trouble you've had, then?"

"Trouble enough." John led the horse to a small pool nearby and let it drink. "But what's done is past. And I think there's others will know the meanin' o' trouble before this matter is ended!"

After a moment he looked around at her. She was still a fetching vision in the moonlight, although Mac-Kenzie thought he rather preferred her hair falling loose about her shoulders, as it had been the night before, to the tight braids she had now worked into it.

"No food, is it?" He grinned. "Well, at least that is somethin' we may be able to remedy, though for reasons I'll explain we dare not risk a fire this night."

He tethered the bay on a small patch of grass beside the ruin, then stood silently looking up at the tall shapes of the trees around them for several minutes. At last he drew his knife and strode into the dark forest without a word. After a time he returned carrying a thick green stalk.

"Cabbage o' the palm," he said when he was beside the girl once more. "Tasty and nourishin' enough, though it barely takes the place of honest meat and bread. But 'twill have to satisfy us both until the morrow, when we may hope to obtain more substantial fare."

While they ate he described the day's happenings in spare language, making no attempt to hide the seriousness of their situation.

"We must leave here without delay," he concluded, "before another day has passed. Beyond that great river to the west of us there is a vast country where we may lose ourselves from any pursuit. Yet without an outfit — powder, shot, a rifle, blankets — 'twill not be an easy journey at the best." He fell silent then, sitting beside her for a long time without speaking. Becky seemed to understand, for she made no attempt to interrupt his thoughts.

Finally MacKenzie rose and stretched, gazing up at the star-filled sky overhead. "Well," he said at last, "there are men about who may trade provisions for a good horse, and we might come to that at the last. But the horse is not mine, and I would not sell it, or keep it, if that can be avoided." He was silent again for a moment.

"What is mine," he said then with grim resolution, "I have no mind to give up without a fight. There is still my outfit at the inn in St. Augustine, a fine Pennsylvania rifle among all the rest. I have a notion to make a try for that before I leave this country." He looked down at the girl beside him.

"I'm afraid it would mean leavin' you alone again for a short while. But if I move quickly I believe I may enter the city and depart again before daylight. Then at least we might be on our way with a bit o' what we'll need." He paused and shrugged. "If I should fail," he said wryly, "you will still be free, and you'll be well mounted for your escape."

She looked up at him, regarding his determined features for a long moment in the moonlight.

"You are a stubborn man, John MacKenzie," she said finally. "And I can see that you're the sort of man as must follow his own mind no matter what the consequences." She drew her thin shawl more tightly about her shoulders and tossed her head so that the moon caught a brief reflection of the resolve in her eyes.

"Yet you must learn," she continued with the barest trace of a smile, "that I am a woman of a similar mind myself. I've no desire at all to be left alone again in this wild place, and I will not be left behind when it's for my sake you're in your present predicament to begin with. Wherever it is that you would go this night, I mean to be going there with you."

MacKenzie opened his mouth to protest, but as he looked into the girl's eyes he suddenly thought better of it. He had seen a bold stubbornness there that more than matched his own. And he knew instinctively he would have little to gain by arguing.

"Very well," he said with a reluctant nod. "If it pleases you, you may come with me as far as the city walls. But then I'll ask you to wait for me outside, for 'twill be stealthy work and dangerous within, and I've a bit more experience at that than you, I think. Nor will there be time to worry about the safety of any but myself."

Becky nodded silently, and with a glance about the clearing John stepped to where the bay stood waiting. "We'd best be on our way then," he said simply, "for this night grows no younger."

6 🌿

UNFASTENING THE ROPE, he took the horse's head and led the way onto a dim trail, different from the path they had used in their earlier approaches. After walking for a short distance John mounted, then reached down and helped Becky up behind him. The bay set out at a brisk pace along the sandy path, between ancient pines and live oaks that loomed huge and ghostlike over their heads.

In less than an hour they were near the city where they could make out the few scattered lights that still burned, as well as those swaying dimly on the masts of ships in the harbor beyond.

Beside the deserted outer wall MacKenzie halted in a thick stand of trees. Dismounting, he helped Becky to the ground, then moved silently to the edge of the woods nearest the earthwork. He studied the scene before them for some time without speaking. At last he turned to the girl.

"I should be gone no more than half an hour," he said, his voice a barely audible whisper. "Do you wait here. If it has been an hour by your reckonin', or if you hear a commotion within the walls before then, do not tarry on my account but mount and ride away as quickly as you can. 'Twill be likely then that I have been taken . . ." He paused, and pointed behind them.

"A short way to the north and west of us is the King's Road. It is the surest route to Georgia, though for that very reason you'll be hard pressed to avoid discovery. Yet if you travel by night, sleep by day, and trust to God's Providence you may win through to safety."

"I will wait" — she met his eyes — "until your return. I've little doubt of it. Then we shall be on our way together into the western wilderness and the lands beyond."

He handed the bay's lead rope to her in silence, and slid over the low rampart to begin his approach to the city. Once across he moved quickly, gliding like a shadow from one patch of concealing brush to another at odd intervals, his senses alert for any sign of activity that might signal the presence of others in the still night.

Entering a field of tall grain some fifty yards from the city, he halted and knelt at a point that gave him a good view of both his own planned path between the hedges and of the guard post on the wall a short distance away to the south.

He saw the sentry lounging within his rough shelter, the glow of his pipe clearly visible in the darkness. It soon became evident that the man was alone. Nor did he seem to have any inclination to leave his meager comfort to walk a deserted post in the small hours of a quiet night.

MacKenzie waited until he was certain of the guard's inactivity. Then he rose and started cautiously forward. He had not taken a half-dozen steps when he froze suddenly, his hand dropping to the hilt of his knife. A shadowy figure had appeared on the wall above the break in the spiny hedge, disappearing from sight a moment later into the ditch beyond.

John knelt where he was, becoming motionless again instantly as he was hidden between the rows of grain. He soon saw the figure reappear, glance quickly at the guard post, and move rapidly away from the wall in a low crouch — directly toward MacKenzie!

The large knife cleared its sheath without a sound. John's muscles tensed briefly and then, deliberately, he forced them to relax. Still he had made no movement that could be detected from even a few feet away.

As the figure came nearer, something about its shape and movement seemed familiar. When familiarity had become recognition, MacKenzie lowered the knife slightly, waiting patiently until the other man was near enough to see him. Then he uttered a low "Ssst!"

Blackie started, froze in his tracks, and turned his body quickly toward the sound. Catching his eye, Mac-Kenzie nodded and motioned with his head that they should withdraw toward the forest without delay. He began moving in that direction, and after hesitating only briefly, the sailor followed.

When they reached a clump of low trees some hundred yards from the guard post, John halted and turned back. He knelt and looked questioningly at the seaman behind him. The other glanced over his shoulder as he came near, then leaned forward and placed his hands on his knees to catch his breath. They had both been moving swiftly.

"Whoosh!" the older man said after a moment, his voice low. "'Tis a greater distance than I've run so quickly this dozen years past! The deck of a ship's a narrow place to stretch your legs, and this is not the sort of exercise I'm accustomed to."

"Aye," John responded, studying his companion. "And an odd time o' the night to begin the practice, I'm thinkin'. What is it that might take you from the soft comforts o' the city at such a cold hour?"

The sailor did not answer immediately. He knelt and

looked at the man beside him. Then he shrugged.

"Some'at the same business I mentioned to you once, perhaps. A desire to see a part of the back country. And it may be this hour's as good as any to begin such a journey." He paused and squinted at the frontiersman. "And what o' yourself?" he asked. "I'd a-thought by now that you'd be halfway to Georgia with your young companion."

"And so we would ha' been," John said grimly, "but for Tyrone's unwanted attentions. Thanks to him I've lost all I had — save the rifle, pack and gelding I left behind at the inn, which I'd plans to recover this night."

Blackie shook his head. "I fear you're to be disappointed in that as well, lad. I heard of your meetin' with Dread Jamie's men on the quay. They arrived at the inn an hour afterward, with a warrant for your arrest sealed by the magistrate's own hand. Your goods have all been seized, and you're a wanted man now — charged wi' theft, assault, resistin' arrest, and a few other crimes I could scarcely cipher the words of. Tyrone has offered a reward for your capture. A hundred guineas, dead or alive." He met the younger man's eyes. "Preferably dead, it is said."

MacKenzie's face darkened. The news was not surprising under the circumstances, but he could have wished the authorities would at least have taken time to investigate the charges before turning a man they did not know into a hunted criminal. There was small chance he would receive a fair trial in this place — or any trial at all, for that matter. A hundred guineas was more than a year's income for an honest tradesman!

He made his decision on the instant. "There is little to keep me here then," he said softly. "So I'd best be on my way without delay." He rose quickly.

The seaman glanced around them, then stood up himself. "I'd go with you a distance," he said, "if you'd not be objectin' to the company. I've no love for Tyrone, nor he for me. And I've at least as much desire to be away from St. Augustine this night as yourself."

John looked at his companion. "I find that last a bit hard to believe. But if you're of the mind, then come along and welcome. The road and forest are open to all."

It took only a few words at their rendezvous to explain the new situation to Becky, and the even more urgent need now for a speedy and secret departure. Then, with the girl mounted on the big bay and Blackie walking beside her, MacKenzie quickly led them north away from the city.

They followed San Sebastian Creek for some distance, crossing it at last at a shallow ford beyond the sight of houses or settlements. There they found a narrow trail that wound westward through the dense pine forests and palmetto thickets east of the St. Johns River.

The woods around them grew darker as the moon dropped below the horizon, but the frontiersman still did not pause nor slow his pace. Finding his way by starlight and memory alone he led them unerringly among huge moss-laden trees and past eerie marshes that frequently bordered their route. More than once they forded narrow creeks overhung by ghostly limbs and vines.

As the sky began to grow pale behind them, John finally left the trail and crossed a low rise, halting at last in a narrow clearing surrounded by oaks, hickories and tall pines. A clear creek ran nearby, its banks thick with reeds and leafy undergrowth.

"We'll pass the day here," he said, helping the girl to the ground. "'Tis but a little farther to the great river, and we daren't risk a crossin' before nightfall. Travelers and fishermen are upon that water at all times, and there are plantations along the shore with a view for miles."

While Becky led the bay to water MacKenzie unsheathed his knife and, with the sailor's help, began fashioning a crude shelter of branches and vines. Once the girl had tethered the big horse where it could reach its fill of grass and tender leaves, John showed his companions how to make a thatch of palmetto fronds, beginning at the bottom and overlapping so that rain would run off it to the ground. He also advised them to dig a shallow ditch around the shelter to keep any runoff water from seeping in. Rain at some time during the day was more likely than not at this season of the year.

When these tasks were well begun John handed his knife to Blackie, turned, and strode silently into the forest. He followed the creek a short way downstream until he found a clear pool, still and deep beneath overhanging limbs. There he removed his boots and waded slowly in up to his waist. He stood without moving and waited patiently while the ripples disappeared and the water became calm once more.

In a few minutes a fat bream appeared, clearly visible beneath the glassy surface. MacKenzie remained motionless while it swam lazily in his direction, circling curiously. As it came nearer he held his breath, then dropped his arms suddenly and with a deft scooping motion lifted the fish from the water and threw it flopping to the near shore.

Again he waited for the pool to become calm. Before long another bream swam into sight. In less than an hour he had caught four more in the same manner.

When he returned to the campsite with his catch the shelter was finished. Giving the fish to his companions to clean, John carefully cleared the leaves from a patch of ground beneath a nearby tree. Then he gathered pine needles, tinder and pieces of dry wood. With sparks from the flintlock on his pistol and his own breath he soon managed to nurse a small fire to life. It was masked by surrounding foliage, and its thin smoke was dissipated by the branches overhead, so that it could not be detected from even a short distance away.

Recovering his knife, he quickly cut and sharpened several green palmetto shafts, stripping them of fronds and setting them into the ground near the fire to broil the fish. Before long a pleasant odor of cooking filled the air of the clearing.

While they ate, MacKenzie sat back against a tree

and studied the seaman across from him with curious eyes. It was not in his nature, nor that of anyone on the frontier, to ask many questions about a man's past or his future plans. If he wanted you to know them he would tell you; and if not, it was clearly none of your business.

Yet there were questions in John's mind that he wanted answers for. Though he'd taken the measure of the sailor the night they'd met and had liked what he'd seen, the situation at the moment called for more than usual caution. MacKenzie would feel more comfortable if he had a better understanding of the other man's motives and intentions. Those might be in harmony with his own and Becky's, but then again they might not.

The older man saw John's eyes upon him, but seemed to pay it little mind as they finished their meal, largely in silence. Afterwards Becky went off a little way to gather branches and leaves for their beds, while MacKenzie spread the coals of the fire and began covering them with sand. The sailor leaned back comfortably on the grass of the clearing and picked his teeth with a fishbone, watching them.

"'Twas a fine breakfast," he observed after a time, "though it's often been said that hunger is the best sauce. A bit o' shut-eye now while the cool o' the day is still on us, and we'll all be ready for what comes." He stretched lazily and waited while MacKenzie finished his task and sat back against the bole of a tree. Then the seaman spoke again:

"What might be your course now, lad?" he asked.

"It's clear you're a fair hand at makin' do in the wilderness. But you've little enough to do with now, I'm thinking. A horse with no saddle. A pistol with no shot or ball. A knife, and only the clothes you're wearin'. It lacks considerable for a journey such as the one you have before you. Especially with a young lady to look after."

John did not reply. He was hearing nothing he had not thought of before this. And he had a feeling the other man was leading up to something.

"When you've seen the lass to safety," Blackie continued, "what then? 'Twill be hard sailin' to return to this colony with Tyrone's men and a warrant waitin' on you, and nothin' o' your own. But return you will, or I've misjudged the kind o' man you are."

"That's all true enough," John replied. "We've little in the way o' supplies, but whatever Providence offers we will make the most of. I've a horse as you say, and there are those who may trade provisions for it and not ask overmany questions. We will have some o' what we need then, and for the rest I can, as you've pointed out, 'make do.'

"For the future, it must take care of itself. I will return here certainly. I've no mind at all to be chased from these Florida lands, by Tyrone or anyone else. And there are some matters to be settled, I think, between myself and that struttin' Irish gamecock — gold or no gold!"

Blackie nodded soberly. "Bold words," he said, "and from another I might have cause to doubt them. Yet I've a thought you're the man to put actions to what you say." He paused, his hand disappearing for a moment beneath the folds of his soiled linen shirt. "But if Providence were, so to speak, lend a helpin' hand, you might not object to the event I'd imagine. You might be inclined to 'make the most of it,' eh?"

He withdrew his hand and suddenly flipped a shining object to the frontiersman, who caught it and raised it between thumb and forefinger. It glittered in the morning sun: a gold coin, thick and heavy, emblazoned with the arms of Spain.

"There is more where that came from," the sailor said. "Much more. A greater treasure than you've imagined in your wildest dreams of avarice, all buried deep beneath these Florida sands!" He glanced at Becky, then looked back at MacKenzie. "More than enough wealth to satisfy the wants o' the three of us for the rest of our natural lives!"

He was staring hard into the frontiersman's eyes. "You take me to that island I spoke of, lad, and I'll show you such riches as you've never dreamed! I know right where it's hidden, and I can take you there straightway if you're o' the mind. What do you say, lad? Share and share alike, the three of us. Is it a bargain?"

MacKenzie made no answer right away. He studied the coin instead, turning it slowly between the fingers of his hand. Then he placed it in his mouth and bit down hard. The metal was soft and heavy: gold, without a doubt.

Finally he raised his eyes to the man across the clearing. The sailor was sitting up cross-legged now, watching him. From his manner it was clear the older man meant both his tale of treasure, and his offer to share it, in deadly earnest. Yet this was far from the first such story of buried gold that John had heard. He knew most of them to be no more than the wishful fantasies of poor and hard-working men — like the one who sat before him now.

"Tell me," MacKenzie asked at last, "what might be the source o' such a treasure as you're speakin' of? And how is it that you might happen to have the knowledge of it, and of its secret hidin' place?"

Blackie met his eyes, then shrugged. "Those are questions I choose not to answer for just now, lad. You must trust me a bit, as I must trust you. I will say only that I do know of a certainty the treasure is there, and that there's no one alive now who has any lawful claim to it, save he who first removes it from the ground."

"And why, then," John's eyes narrowed, "would you be willin' to share it wi' the two of us?"

The sailor shrugged again. "I'm o' the sea, lad. I know naught of the forests and the fens and the beasts in this treacherous land. 'Twould be folly for me to attempt such a quest alone. I need the help of a man like yourself, a man who knows this country as well as I know the blue waters." He glanced from one to the other of his companions.

"And I'm not a greedy man, neither. All I want's a

small tavern somewhere, snug and shipshape by the water's edge, and a bit o' somethin' put by for my old age. More than that would only lead to evil — from them as'd have the gold from me, or from my own folly. There's enough for all, and more. You've both as much use for it as I, so why not share? The lass can purchase her indenture back, you can invest in land, livestock, commercial ventures or whatever you will. And there's that left over which might serve to help us give Tyrone a proper settlement, in his own coin."

MacKenzie regarded the other man thoughtfully. Then he spoke again:

"You've mentioned trust, yet it seems to me it's a dangerous secret you're sharin' wi' two strangers. Why should you put your faith in a man like myself, whom you've only just met?" He nodded in Becky's direction. "Or in the lass, for that matter? What's to prevent the one or the both of us from leaving your bones by the wayside and takin' it all for ourselves, now or later?"

"For the now," Blackie responded with a sly grin, "the answer's simple enough. You'd gain nothing at all for your trouble but the one coin I've already given you for the purchase of an outfit. I've no more with me. And you'll never find the rest without my help. 'Tis an island like many others where the treasure lies buried, and no map of it in all the world but here." He tapped his head with a forefinger.

"As for the later, well . . ." The sailor narrowed his eyes, looking from the frontiersman to the girl and back again. "I have seen a bit o' the world in my forty-odd years, lad. I've known a few men and I've the feelin' for what's inside of 'em. You and the lass, now. I'd say you'll do for loyal shipmates, come fair weather or foul." He lay back on his elbows and his grin broadened.

"O' course, I *might* be wrong. But then I reckon I'll take my chances. Old Blackie's no babe in arms. He's weathered a storm or two here and there, and he's still around to tell the tale of it!"

John looked hard at the seaman. Then he nodded. "Aye, and I've no doubt o' that. I do believe you're a man, as they say in the western lands, to ride the river with." He turned to Becky, who was sitting quietly nearby.

"But what do you say, lass? I'll confess I might find the prospect temptin' myself, seein' that I've little to lose in any case. But it's not my choice to make. I promised I'd see you safely to the country in the north, and I'd not change our course unless you wished it. 'Tis a dangerous chance we'd be taking, make no mistake about it. A long hard journey at the very least. It might mean riches, or it might mean death in the wilderness. Or again, it might mean nothin' at all to show for all our strivin' and our difficulties."

There was no hesitation in Becky's reply.

"I've known difficulties before," she said quietly, "and hard journeys and striving, too. And little else from the time I was old enough to hold a carder and a laundry board. I'd nothing in the old country. No family, no fortune, and no prospects. That's why I indentured myself and took passage to this new land, for the opportunity to better myself. An opportunity is all I've ever asked of this world, and it seems to me this is one."

She threw back her head and stared boldly at her companions. "If we began with nothing and have gained nothing, then we have lost nothing at all, have we? I say seize the main chance, and let come what may!"

There was a moment of silence. Then Blackie slapped his knees with both hands. "Now there's a lass!" he exclaimed. He looked at John. "It's agreed, then?"

"Aye." MacKenzie nodded. "Agreed. We will leave this night, after a good day's rest and whatever provisionin' I can manage wi' the help o' your gold." He held out a hand to the girl, and his other to the seaman.

"All share and share alike," he said, "come what will." As they clasped hands, he could not help adding: "And confusion to our enemies, whoever and wherever they may be!"

7

JAMES TYRONE STOOD STIFFLY, gazing out from the second-story balcony of his townhouse across the narrow streets of the city to the harbor beyond. He was not in a pleasant mood.

His hand hurt abominably, and he had not slept well. Word of the frontiersman's escape the night before had been followed this morning by a report of the disappearance of a certain old sea dog from the *posada,* and apparently from the city as well — a man Tyrone had not known until that instant was within a thousand miles of St. Augustine.

He had men on the quay now, to discover if the sailor had taken passage on any of the ships lying at anchor in Matanzas Inlet. But he had a strong suspicion that was not the case. Old Blackie had been staying at the same inn as that man MacKenzie. Supposing they had met, and talked? Supposing . . . ?

He smote the balustrade with his good hand and began to pace catlike, up and down the narrow loggia. The girl was an impudent baggage who had wounded his pride, the frontiersman a bold vagabond with an inflated idea of his own importance. After what had happened the past two nights Tyrone would take grim pleasure in running both to ground and destroying them. Yet he was realist enough to know that even their escape, if it happened, would pose no real threat to his plans in East Florida.

Blackpool Bobbie's presence here was another matter entirely.

There was a footstep on the stairs within. Tyrone halted his restless pacing and turned to face the doorway. A moment later Jack Thatcher appeared, ducking his head as he passed through the low archway onto the balcony. His scarred face was flushed with running the hundred yards from the harbor.

"Not a sign of the ol' dog," he said with a shake of his head. "Came in aboard the *Mary Ellen* three days ago, took his pay, and has not been seen on the waterfront since. The landlord at the inn says he settled his account yesterday, and was gone before breakfast. No one's seen him at all since last night."

Tyrone nodded. He must assume the worst then, that MacKenzie and the sailor had somehow managed to join forces. It might not be so, and he would have his men search for Blackie in more likely spots as well. But if those two were together . . .

"Jack, my boyo," he said in a low voice. "It is a job I have for you, and a few other tight-lipped men. It is a job that I would not want mentioned where curious ears might hear, now or later." He paused, glancing beyond the taller man into the building, then over his own shoulder toward the street.

"That frontiersman, MacKenzie. I want him pursued, Jack. I want him found, no matter where he may be hidin' in the wilderness. And when he is found, Jack lad, then I want him dead. And the same for any other man who might happen to be travelin' with him. Am I makin' myself clear to you?"

"Aye." Thatcher nodded, his own voice low. "Clear enough. It's that much I owe the man myself." He paused. "And what of the girl, then?"

"The girl." Tyrone smiled. "The girl indeed. I would have Miss Campbell brought back here, Jack, to remain under my own roof. For a time, at least." The smile disappeared as he returned his thoughts to the matter at hand.

"You will take Bill Simms with you, and long-knife Ben Pike, and the native for the trackin'" — the Irishman's blue eyes narrowed slightly — "yet I still do not trust that savage completely." He thought for a minute. "There is a man with a cabin near the road to Rolles Town, a few leagues to the south. His name is LeBeau. A half-breed, I think. D'ye know him?"

"Aye, I know him. A smuggler, a stealer of cattle, a sometime highwayman. A hard man."

"A man who has lived his life in the wilderness entirely, I'm told. A tracker and a long hunter without peer. I would have you visit LeBeau this night, Jack, with word of the hundred guineas reward. You are to offer it to him, all of it, for his help in runnin' our quarry to the ground."

"All of it?" The tall man looked at Tyrone with raised eyebrows.

"You are to offer it to him, Jack. All of it. When the job is properly done, then you are to pay him. In cold steel."

Thatcher looked doubtful. "That may be some simpler said than done, Cap'n. 'Tis a hard man there, as I say. A very hard man. Nor one I'd want to trust a girl to whom I'd future plans for, if you know what I mean. I would not leave them together for even an hour was I you. Not if you'd want her back in undamaged condition, so to speak!"

"Then you will not leave them alone together, Jack, will you?" Tyrone spoke calmly. "You will keep a weather eye on the situation, and you will be sure to pay LeBeau in full just as soon as our frontiersman is found." He placed a hand on the other's shoulder. "I know you will find the way, Jack. It's that much faith I have in you."

The Irishman turned his back to his companion, clasping his hands behind him as he looked out once more across the harbor. "Do you see to gatherin' the others now, and make ready to leave first thing in the morning. Then go yourself this night to LeBeau's cabin to offer him our proposition. And Jacko . . ."

The tall man paused in the doorway.

"See that you do not come upon MacKenzie and his party too close to the settlements, eh? I have gained some bit of influence in this colony, but I'd still not want the manner of their deaths to become widely known. It would be far more . . . convenient . . . if they were to simply disappear in the wilderness without a trace!"

The rain began with a few large drops, spattering intermittently on the palmetto shelter overhead. Then it came with a sudden rush, driving straight down in torrents that drenched the grass of the clearing and quickly filled the shallow ditch around the lean-to where MacKenzie and his companions slept. Low thunder rumbled in the distance.

John's eyes opened and he lay still, gazing up at the yellow-green fronds and listening until the afternoon downpour spent its initial force and slackened to a steady drumming. Soon he heard his companions stir, and raised himself up on one elbow.

Becky, who had half risen at the sound of the storm, glanced around and met MacKenzie's eyes. Then she curled up again on her leafy pallet, drawing her shawl more tightly about her head and shoulders to ward off the occasional drops that fell from the thatch overhead. The old sailor still appeared to be sleeping soundly, but as John watched he saw Blackie's fingers did not relax their grip on the hilt of the knife at his side.

Stretching, MacKenzie lay back with his hands beneath his head, thinking about his comrades and the journey that lay before them. He was pleased with what he'd seen of Blackie so far — including the fact that despite appearances the older man was clearly a light sleeper, and he kept his weapons close to hand. It was the sign of a careful man.

John had never depended on the vigilance and fighting ability of others, even when he'd been among more able comrades than himself. The strongest man was the one who stood alone, and there was danger in counting too heavily on someone else to do what you should do yourself.

Still, it would make his task easier not to have to be constantly watching over his friends in the wilderness. There was much in this Florida land that was foreign, even to men who had spent a lifetime on the frontiers to the north and west. The dangers were many, and MacKenzie knew he would have to be a teacher as well as a guide if they were all to reach the west coast of the peninsula safely. That was why Blackie's natural instinct for caution and his vigilance were comforting. It suggested he might make a good student.

Nor did John have many doubts about Becky on that score. She was a country lass, knowledgeable of the ways of animals and growing things, and she had proven herself quick to learn. The girl was a hard worker too, always willing to do her share and a bit more.

The rain seemed to be slackening. It was almost a daily occurrence at this time of the year, but seldom lasted more than an hour or two. With luck it would be over well before nightfall. John hoped to make arrangements for what they needed quickly so they could cross the St. Johns River after dark and be far from the nearest settlements by morning.

He had an idea where he might get the provisions and the boat they would need for the first leg of their journey. Few Britons who had received grants from the Crown had actually settled on their spacious Florida estates. Most employed overseers to manage their property, very often colonials like himself.

The plantations these men controlled were as self-sufficient as any feudal manor. Most of what was needed was produced on the premises, and what could not be produced or obtained by barter was done without. There was little use for governments of any sort. Like men on the frontier everywhere the overseers were tough, independent men, well accustomed to relying on their own resources. For one of their own — and a Spanish piece of gold — they would willingly provide whatever they could spare with few questions asked.

MacKenzie knew one such man, a Carolinian like himself, and a former comrade in arms during the Cherokee Wars. He was employed by the absentee landlord to manage a plantation only a few miles from their present camp.

When the rain had subsided, John took up his knife and pistol and crawled to the entrance of their makeshift shelter. With a whispered word to his comrades he stepped out into the dripping clearing. The sky was the color of burnished copper as he brushed water from the back of the big bay and mounted. Turning the horse's head to the northwest he rode off into the gathering twilight at a steady trot.

In less than an hour he was near the plantation compound. Dismounting and picketing the bay among some trees a quarter of a mile distant, John advanced to where he could see the buildings without being observed himself. Then he stood in the shadows for a time, watching the lights come on in the small settlement. The slaves were in from the fields by now, and most of them were in their rough cabins behind the main house preparing for supper. He saw no movement at all except the thin rising columns of smoke from a dozen cook-fires.

Satisfied finally that there was nothing out of the ordinary about this peaceful scene, he entered the yard and began to approach the big two-story structure. As he stepped up onto the porch he moved to one side of the door, then knocked gently. After a moment it opened and a dark-haired young woman stood framed in the rectangle of light, peering out into the growing darkness.

"Yes? Who is it? Oh, John! This is a surprise!" She took his hands warmly. "We'd no idea you were even in the neighborhood. Come in, come in!"

"Evenin', Molly. Sorry to come callin' unannounced at this hour o' the night, but I've an urgent need to speak with Robert if he's about." MacKenzie stepped into the spotless hallway and removed his hat. "It's a matter o' some importance, and I'm afraid I've no time for a proper visit." He glanced into the two adjoining rooms as the girl closed the door behind them. "I'd as soon no others knew that I was about," he said quietly, "if y'don't mind."

"Secret business, is it?" She looked up at him, her eyes twinkling. "And what sort o' turmoil is it that you've got yourself into now, I wonder?" John smiled at her, but said nothing.

"Ah, so I am right, then? No matter. You menfolk may have your secrets, but I will find out all in my own time!" She winked, then said more seriously, "You've no cause to worry, for Mary's in the kitchen out back, and there's no one in the house now but father and myself. Do you wait there in the library while I fetch him." She started down the hallway before turning back.

"D'you care for a spot of tea? I've just put the kettle on."

"Thank you, Molly. I would take a cup if it's no

trouble." He stepped into the small bookshelf-lined office and closed the door behind him. A few minutes later it swung open again and a large ruddy-faced man of forty years entered the room.

"John MacKenzie!" the man said warmly, taking the frontiersman's hand in a viselike grip. "'Tis a pleasure to see you, lad! I'd no idea you were about this part o' the country at all!"

"I've been in the wilderness, Robert, trappin' furs for trade. I'd only just returned two days ago, and had no chance to call on you. For it seems . . ." He fell silent as Molly appeared, carrying a tray.

The girl set the tea things down on a small table and started out, but paused in the doorway, looking back curiously. When MacKenzie shook his head she winked at him, then turned with a saucy flip of her skirt and closed the door behind her.

"It's been some years, Robert," John said when they were alone again. "More than I'd thought till I saw Molly just now. She's grown into a lovely young woman."

"She has that." The large man took a seat and began to pour two cups of tea. "And along with it, all the worries and troubles that fact brings to a widowed father. There's hardly a day passes now some young man's not hoverin' about our door, makin' cow eyes and offerin' his services for this and that and the other thing." He shook his head and handed a cup to his guest.

As MacKenzie seated himself and took a sip of tea, the older man looked at him closely. "It's pleased I am to see you John, always. But Molly tells me that you have not come merely on a social call . . ."

"Aye, I'm afraid I have not." John met the other man's eyes. "It's trouble, Robert, and I've landed myself squarely in the thick of it — though from no design o' my own. I've the need to make my way into the back country again this very night, with my two companions. I'd hopes you might be able to help me with a boat, an outfit and a few provisions. I'm able to pay for the favor, as it turns out . . . ."

He reached into his jacket and produced Blackie's gold coin. The overseer took it and turned it over in his fingers. He looked curiously at his visitor.

"I can tell you nothing o' that," John said seriously. "And little else besides. Save that I'm a hunted man with a warrant and a price on my head. I only mention that much so you'll know the risk you'll be takin' in comin' to my aid." He took another swallow of tea, then looked over the cup at his host. "I'd be understandin' if you refused, though I'd hoped you might not for old times' sake."

"'Old times' sake,' he says!" Dropping the coin to the table, the large man ran his fingers through his thinning blond hair. "And do you think I'd be forgettin' that but for you this ragged scalp would even now be adornin' the lodge pole o' some red devil's wickiup? Robert Fleming is not the man to forget that kind of a debt!" He downed his tea and rose from his chair.

"If the goods were mine alone to give I'd shove that

coin down your throat for even offerin' it! Yet since they're only mine in trust I'll accept your money, with thanks. But for the rest, do not give it another thought. Name your needs — anything at all — and it's yours!"

It took only a few minutes for John to describe their situation, and the supplies they would need for the trek through the wilderness. He ignored his friend's raised eyebrows at the request for women's clothing and comfortable walking shoes, thanking his good fortune that Robert Fleming was both a discreet and a trusting man.

Arrangements were made quickly for blankets, ammunition, food and other provisions from the plantation's stores, and a small sailing boat was available for transportation as well. The clothing required a bit more thought, however, for Becky was some several inches taller than Molly's five-one. But at last the overseer recalled a trunk that had belonged to his late wife, and upon inspection John decided that some of the articles in it would do well enough.

When instructions for gathering the supplies and loading the boat had been entrusted to a reliable servant, John and his host spent a brief half hour and a glass of sherry catching up on the events of the past several years. At last MacKenzie rose and extended his hand.

"My thanks for your help, Robert. I'll not be forgettin' it. Now I must be off, for we've a need to be some miles beyond the river come daybreak."

Fleming took the offered hand in both of his own, looking seriously into his friend's eyes. "You keep well,

John MacKenzie. And if I can help any in the future, you let me know. I've a few connections in the Mother Country that might prove useful. And I'll send word to your family in any event. A warrant's but a piece o' paper that may need only the right other piece o' paper to overcome.

"In the meantime" — he winked — "do not concern yourself overmuch about this visit, for I find my memory already beginnin' to fail me!"

He led John to the outer door, but as he laid a hand on the latch a sound outside made MacKenzie grasp his friend's arm and place an urgent finger to his lips.

"Horses!" he whispered after a moment. "A half-dozen or more!"

8 🗲

MACKENZIE LOOKED AT FLEMING. "Are you expectin' visitors?" he asked.

The other man shook his head. "None at this time o' the night." He was whispering also. "Mayhap they're huntin' you. — Quick! Out through the back o' the house and into the trees beyond! We'll keep them occupied till you're safely away!"

As the horsemen drew rein in the front yard, Mac-

Kenzie moved rapidly down the hallway to the back door. There he paused, peering out through the small side window. Two riders were already walking their mounts into the moonlit enclosure. The house was surrounded.

Glancing over his shoulder, John saw a narrow flight of stairs a few feet away. Without hesitating he wheeled and took the steps two at a time, moving lightly on his toes so as to make no sound. When he reached the landing he could hear voices in the hallway below. One of them he recognized as that of Tyrone's 'Captain of Light Horse,' the man who called himself Bonneville Richards.

"I must apologize for the inconvenience we've caused in coming here at this hour of the night," Richards was saying, "but there is an escaped felon abroad in the countryside, and we've orders to search all the plantations in the vicinity. I doubt he's nearby, yet the man is dangerous, and so we must leave no stone unturned."

Fleming spoke briefly, followed by Molly. MacKenzie could not make out their words, but Richards' reply could be heard clearly:

"I understand entirely. But our instructions are to search every building. However, I will keep my men outside. While they have a look about the grounds and the slave quarters, I'll take a quick turn through the house myself. With your permission, Miss Molly? Sir?"

John did not wait to hear more. He quickly entered the darkened bedroom on his left, closing the door behind him and stepping to the open window across the room. At Richards' orders most of the riders were moving off now toward the slave cabins and the other outbuildings. One man remained in view, but for the moment his back was turned to the house.

The stairs creaked, and MacKenzie placed a foot on the windowsill. There were no trees nearby, but looking up he could see a thick beam supporting the deep overhang of the roof. It was some four feet away. Glancing behind him he saw a flickering light appear at the crack beneath the bedroom door. There was no more time for thought. John stood on the sill, leaned out to grasp the exposed rafter, and pulled himself upward.

It was a tight fit, but he was able to loop an arm over the beam and hold himself there by bracing his feet hard against the clapboard wall of the house. He managed to get himself situated an instant before the door opened and Richards strode into the bedroom with a lighted taper.

John gritted his teeth against the effort of remaining still while the muscles of his legs strained to hold his position. The captain took several minutes examining the room, but at last he moved on, closing the door softly behind him.

Keeping his eyes on the rider below, who fortunately had still not turned toward the house, MacKenzie lowered himself slowly and carefully back to the windowsill. It was no easy task, for the distance was too far for comfort, and he could afford no misstep. His legs were trembling when he finally stepped into the room and could kneel to catch his breath. Still he was grateful that Richards had no reason to know of his connection with the overseer of this plantation, for the captain's inspection of the premises had been only a cursory one.

In a few minutes all the riders had returned to the house, and after Richards spoke to them briefly from the front porch, John raised his head cautiously to look out the window and saw them moving away at a brisk trot — on their way, he supposed, to the next plantation. He rose and crossed quickly to the bedroom door.

As his hand grasped the latch he halted and swore suddenly under his breath. Bonneville Richards' voice could be heard clearly from the parlor at the front of the house:

"I could not help but notice that you had tea made, Miss Molly. If you would not mind greatly, I would tarry a moment to join you in a cup. It is not often a man in my profession has the opportunity to enjoy the company of so lovely a lady."

For a brief instant MacKenzie considered returning downstairs and entering the parlor. He would like to see Richards' expression when they met, and he relished the prospect of facing the captain man-to-man without his troopers to back him up. But that would only bring trouble to Fleming and his daughter, and John owed them much for their help this night. Besides, there was no time to be lost if he and his companions were to make their escape across the river before daylight.

With a regretful shake of his head John dismissed the thought and returned to the windowsill. He looked cautiously out. There was no one in sight. Swinging a leg over, he lowered himself gradually until his weight was held only by his fingertips. Then he released them and dropped without a sound onto the soft grass beside the house. As he was moving away into the shadows he could still hear Richards' voice, striving to impress the overseer's daughter with tales of his manly accomplishments.

John found the sound more than a little annoying under the circumstances. He ought to do something, he reflected, to at least take that polished ruffian down a notch or two before leaving this place. He considered the possibilities while he returned to the spot where he had tied the bay.

The horse had been well concealed and had remained undetected during the troopers' hasty search. Now John removed the halter and rope, slapped the animal gently on the rump, and watched as it trotted quickly off into the forest. He'd no further need for it now, and had no desire to add a real horse theft to the trumped-up charges Tyrone had already laid at his door. The bay would probably find its own way home by morning.

MacKenzie smiled to himself then, as he turned toward the plantation house and began making a slow and stealthy approach back to the place where Richards' gelding stood calmly cropping grass in the moonlight.

Stepping lightly, like an Indian, he came up to the horse and placed a hand on its neck, whispering gently in its ear. Then he reached down and plucked a few coarse stalks from the ground nearby, lifted the blanket and pushed them carefully up beneath the saddle. His knife flashed briefly in the pale light. In seconds Mac-Kenzie was moving swiftly away toward the river, silent as a ghost.

He regretted the momentary pain the hard sandspurs under the saddle would cause the animal, but it was a small price for the humbling effect they were likely to have on his pompous master. Especially when the half-cut cinch gave way and landed Tyrone's Captain of Light Horse unceremoniously on his backside.

The moon was high by the time MacKenzie returned to the campsite, throwing the shapes of the trees along his path into deep relief. He carried a small pack on his back now, together with a dozen arrows in a quiver. A water bottle hung at his side and an Indian bow was in his left hand.

The pistol in his belt had been cleaned and oiled, and it was freshly charged. No matter how pressed for time, it would never have occurred to John to postpone these tasks. Caring for one's weapons was an unshakable habit in the wilderness, a matter of simple survival.

Halting in the shadows beyond the clearing, he called out softly to his companions. When they replied he approached and removed the pack, taking out two small bundles of meat and bread, wrapped in cloth.

"A cold supper," he said, handing the food to Blackie and the girl, "but we cannot risk a fire this night. Our pursuers are about, and restless it seems. When you've eaten we'll be on our way across the river. 'Tis my hope to be well beyond it by the dawnin'."

The sailor unwrapped his supper and took a bite, eyeing MacKenzie's pack suspiciously. "That seems right small provisions, lad, for a coin o' gold." He spoke between mouthfuls. "I trust there's more?"

"Aye. We've everything that's needed for our journey I think — save a rifle, which was not to be had. It is all aboard the boat, a short way downstream."

He took out another bundle and then reshouldered his pack. "The bay horse is on its way home. I would not want to give the impression among certain thieves and renegades that I am of their kind. And in any event we'll travel faster by water on the first leg of our trek. Nor leave any trail for those who might follow after."

When the sailor and the girl had eaten, John handed Becky the clothes and shoes he had obtained from his friend, together with a woolen jacket to ward off the night's chill. As soon as she had donned these he led his companions westward, following the course of the stream that ran beside their camp. They made no effort to strike their makeshift shelter or conceal their campsite, for a good tracker coming upon the spot would hardly be fooled in any case, and by morning the three would be miles away.

❖   ❖   ❖

After half an hour of walking they came to the mouth of the creek where it entered a broad waterway, fifty yards wide and shimmering in the moonlight. Beneath low-hanging branches nearby a narrow punt was moored, well-stocked with provisions and with a short mast and sail at its center. It took only minutes for the three companions to climb aboard and push off from shore.

Using a long pole, MacKenzie maneuvered the craft into the slow-moving current. Then, laying the pole down beside them in the boat, he took hold of the tiller as Blackie began working the sheets to catch the easterly breeze. Soon they were running before the wind, their wake spreading in silver ripples behind them.

The waterway opened into a broad bay of the St. Johns, and after another hour they were well into the channel of the great river, making good speed with the aid of both wind and current. MacKenzie was steering northwestward toward a jut of land on the far shore, dimly seen as a dark line several miles away.

Rounding this promontory they passed the wide mouth of a creek on their left, clearly visible in the moonlight. Two miles farther on they came to a second tributary entering the great river from the west. With a word to Blackie, John turned the rudder and they put into this broad opening between tree-topped bluffs which towered high above them.

Here their progress slowed, for they were traveling

upstream and had to stay closer to the shoreline to avoid the strongest currents. Cypress, laurel and a profusion of lesser flora lined the creek, enfolding its banks in deep shadow. On the bluffs over their heads huge live oaks seemed to reach out grasping arms toward them. MacKenzie raised his eyes to the star-filled sky. It was after midnight.

He spoke to Becky and motioned her aft. Climbing gingerly from her position in the bow, the girl made her way over the bundles and Blackie's compact body until she was able to change places with the frontiersman at the helm. He took her hand and laid it on the tiller, then moved forward with equal care.

"Keep her steady and this far from the shore always," he said. "The river's deep here and there's small danger o' goin' aground, though it will curve and bend." He took the ropes from Blackie's hands and motioned him forward.

"Do you get some rest now," he said to the sailor. "I mean to stay upon the water as long as we're able, to reduce the chances o' pursuit — though I hardly expect it this far from the settlements. But we'll not make camp until we have reached the shallows, sometime tomorrow afternoon."

Jacob LeBeau was a large man, taller by two inches than tall Jack Thatcher and outweighing him by easily a hundred pounds. Nor was there a single ounce of softness in his huge frame. He was a man of great appetites and few restraints, accustomed from long habit to taking whatever was needed to satisfy his hungers of the moment. So far in his life he'd had little difficulty in satisfying them all.

LeBeau would never be considered a thoughtful man, though not lacking in a certain native cunning. Yet he was thinking now. The offer Thatcher had just made him was tempting. A hundred guineas to trail a man and come upon him in the wilderness. It was a fortune for what to LeBeau was the simplest of tasks. And LeBeau found himself wondering why.

"MacKenzie," he said slowly. "I know him. A strong man. Knows the wilderness well."

Thatcher was becoming uncomfortable under the other man's gaze. He averted his eyes and glanced about the dirty cabin.

"That is why we have come to you," he said, forcing confidence into his voice. "You know the wilderness yourself, and you're also a strong man. If anyone could find him out there, you can."

"I can find him. When I find him, then what?"

"I pay you. You leave. Come back here, or go wherever you want."

"Find him. Leave. That's all?"

"That's all." Thatcher allowed himself a brief smile. "It will be enough."

"He is alone in the wilderness?" LeBeau's yellow eyes narrowed slyly.

"There may be another man with him. A man of the

sea, no frontiersman." Thatcher hesitated. "And a woman, perhaps. Neither is any concern of yours."

The large man's eyes kindled briefly with a hunger he had not felt for a long while. A woman. A white woman? He wanted to know more, but he'd seen the doubt — fear? — in his visitor's eyes. He said only:

"I will find them. This man MacKenzie and his party."

9 🌾

IT WAS WELL PAST MIDAFTERNOON when John and his companions finally put into shore. For several hours the fork of the creek they were following had grown steadily narrower and more densely overhung with low branches. Finally they had been forced to un-step the mast and make their way with pole and oars alone.

They had been moving southward for the past half

hour or so, and the open place where they landed on the west bank was covered with high grass sloping up to the bare crest of a hill some three-quarters of a mile away. Beyond this rise could be seen the tops of tall pine trees. The opposite shore was a steep bluff densely overgrown with many varieties of trees and shrubs.

"We will leave the boat here," John said, "and must travel on foot for some distance now. The next waterway is too far for a portage, I fear."

With help from the others he began organizing their supplies into three packs that could be carried easily, with several larger bundles left over. After disembarking Blackie and Becky with all the supplies on the western side, John poled across to the east bank and dragged the punt from the water. Overturning it, he carefully hid the craft beneath branches and low brush. Then he recrossed the stream to join his companions.

He led them partway up the slope, halting beside a huge and solitary live oak tree. At its base they buried the larger bundles, wrapping the supplies in heavy oilcloth first. It could not hurt to have such a cache awaiting their return, for there was no telling what might befall in the meantime.

Changing to a spare pair of moccasins from his pack, MacKenzie hung his damp boots about his neck by a rawhide thong. Then he started through the tall grass, climbing steadily toward the crest of the hill with Blackie and the girl following close behind.

After a short distance the meadow ended and they

found themselves at the edge of a great forest of huge long-leaf pines towering hundreds of feet over their heads. Some of the trunks were so large that a man could not reach around them with both arms. As they stepped into this welcome shade a kind of stillness enfolded them, broken only now and then by the rat-tat-tat of a solitary woodpecker and the gentle humming of cicadas in the distance.

John smiled inwardly as he watched the effect on his companions. He knew their feelings, for they were much the same as his own. There was a rare kind of peace here among the great trees, amid the sparse undergrowth and broad shadowed aisles thickly carpeted over with pine needles and wiregrass. It gave one a sense of reverence almost, so that visitors walked softly and spoke in whispers even though the nearest of their kind might be miles away. MacKenzie took pleasure in sharing this bit of grandeur with those who traveled with him.

After another hour of steady walking they halted in the forest and made camp. They had brought with them a canvas tarpaulin which could be quickly rigged into a lean-to with a part of the material folded under for a ground covering. While Becky gathered pine needles and stuffed them beneath the fabric for a bed, John started a fire fueled by the abundant dead-falls which lay everywhere about them. With his friends' help, a supper of bacon and corn cakes was soon made ready, and a small pot of water for tea was left heating in the coals.

Blackie spent a few minutes gathering additional

wood for the fire. Then he sat down against the bole of a nearby tree and removed his shoes. He wriggled his toes gratefully through the holes in his tattered woolen stockings.

"This trekin' through the wilderness for hours on end is not an easy thing for an old sailor-man to take," he said after a moment. "Not that I'm complainin', mind you. The journey's my own idea, and it's my own feet must bear the cost of it. Yet steady walking upon the hard ground has seldom been my chosen means o' travel. It will take a bit of gettin' used to."

"Aye," MacKenzie replied. "And that is why newcomers such as yourself are called 'tenderfeet' on the frontier." He indicated one of the packs. "You'll find a spare pair o' stockins or two in there. Change them often, for you must keep your feet dry or suffer mightily from blisters." He nodded toward the seaman's shoes. "And whenever you remove your boots, be sure always to shake them out before puttin' them on again. Scorpions and other crawlin' creatures have a great fondness for the warmth and the darkness."

He saw Becky shudder as she knelt by the fire. "Aye, lass, it does take a bit o' thinkin' and plannin' to live in the wilderness. You must consider much that those across the water in England have forgotten or never knew. Yet 'tis a simpler life in many ways." He smiled. "There are no warrants here, nor magistrates. No kings, no Parliaments, no taxes. And the only source o' justice for a man is that which he makes himself. The real law in the forest here, is the universal law o' the wild."

"A harsh law that is," Becky said, pulling the teapot from the coals with two sticks, "it seems to me. The punishment for simple ignorance and carelessness in this wilderness might be death!"

"It might," John conceded. "But is that not always the way? In Europe for a poor man to shoot a deer out of need or ignorance carries the same penalty. And many a stranger in the streets o' London or Marseilles has paid a price in blood for somethin' he did not know of or plan for. No matter where a man lives, I believe the crimes of ignorance and carelessness have always found such means to exact their punishment."

"That's true," Blackie agreed, "for I've seen it often enough myself. Yet in this Florida land we are like babes, the lass and I. We know naught of its laws, nor its many dangers. It is somethin' to be considered."

"Aye." John glanced from one to the other. "It is, and I know it. I will teach you what I can as we travel. But you must learn to see with your own eyes too. And you must always be prepared to think before you act. I could never hope in such a short time to have you ready for every unexpected event."

When they had eaten John took up his bow and arrows, intending to do some hunting while it was still light. Their supply of food was limited by what they could carry, and it would not last the entire journey. Besides, he always preferred fresh meat to salt pork and jerked beef.

By following the natural slope of the ground he soon came upon a small stream. A short way along it he found a narrow ford with sandy banks that contained many signs of game. Moving in a wide circle until he was downwind of the spot, he concealed himself carefully and waited. It was not long before a family of deer appeared for their evening drink.

As the buck and two does approached the water, John rose silently from the bushes, one arrow nocked on his bowstring and a second in his left hand. He took aim at the buck, took a breath and held it, then loosed the shaft. It went true, striking the animal between the shoulder blades near the heart. The second arrow took the creature in the side as it leapt, and a moment later MacKenzie was splashing through the stream in hot pursuit.

It was not a long chase, for either wound would have been enough to kill. In a few minutes John had cleaned and skinned his catch, and was preparing the best cuts to wrap in the skin for his return to camp. He should be there well before dark. There was no need for further hunting this day; he knew that no matter where they traveled in the Florida wilderness there would be little shortage of game.

On his way back he stopped to drink at the stream and to fill the water bottle at his side. As he started to rise, his attention was suddenly caught by a shallow depression in the soft earth a few feet away. It was indistinct among the fallen leaves and grass on the bank, yet its shape and appearance were somehow different from that of a wild animal.

Rising carefully, without moving his feet, he studied the ground for a long time in a widening circle around him. A little way downstream he saw another, similar, depression. He moved slowly toward it, his eyes constantly searching the soft earth, and came to a place where the bank had been caved in a short while before. Beyond that was a patch of bare sand.

Here the sign was clear enough: a footprint, a bare foot. There was another a short way farther on, half in and half out of the water. From their size, depth and the length of stride, John judged they were the prints of a man of slightly less than average height and build. And he could also tell that they had been made recently, almost certainly within the last two hours.

An Indian? Possible, but hardly likely. The Florida natives generally wore moccasins or deerskin boots. The bare foot seemed to rule out a white man as well, for none of them would be willing to brave the cactus, nettles and sandspurs of this land without footwear of some kind. A man who traveled through it without shoes would do so only because he had no shoes to wear.

Studying the print, MacKenzie nodded finally to himself. There was one likely possibility, and only one that he could think of: an escaped slave.

Slowly raising his eyes to the forest around him, he looked carefully again in all directions. He took his time, moving only his head and using the corners of his eyes to detect any movement. He saw nothing.

That suited John, for he had no desire to hinder such a poor soul in his desperate attempt at freedom. Let him live out his life in the wild if he could, or let him join forces with the Indians if he and they were of a mind. There was room enough in this frontier land for all.

Still, the man's presence was something to be considered. For many black slaves had been warriors in their own country, and they'd been given little reason to love any white man on this side of the water. The mere fact that MacKenzie and his party had food and weapons might be reason enough for an attack.

Moreover, the loss of such a valuable item of property would likely prompt a pursuit by the man's owners or their agents before much more time had passed. Slave hunters were generally known for their cruelty and ruthlessness, as well as the tenacity with which they stalked their human prey.

All things considered, John had no wish to encounter the hunters or the hunted in this case. He and his companions must be doubly on their guard now, and they must move swiftly on the morrow in order to put as much distance between themselves and this location as possible.

Having come to that conclusion MacKenzie wasted no more time beside the stream. He shouldered his skin full of meat and took another careful look in all directions, then made his way quickly back to camp.

Arriving at twilight, John explained in a few words what he had found, and the added need for vigilance on all their parts. While he hung up the venison to cool in the night air, he had his friends scatter the coals of their fire and cover them well with sand. The warmth was not needed at this time of the year, and even a faint glow might well be seen for miles in the wilderness.

In the daylight that remained John cleaned and checked his weapons, recharging his pistol from one of several powder horns they had brought with them, and then advising Blackie to do the same. The moist climate meant there was always a danger the powder in their weapons might lose its potency in a matter of days or even hours. Afterwards he sent his companions off to sleep, preferring to stand the first watch himself. He wanted time to think about this latest development, and to plan for the days ahead.

He woke from habit in the first cold light before dawn. The night had passed without incident. Remaining motionless in his blankets for several minutes, John listened to the morning sounds. When he finally rolled over and began to get up he was pleased to see Blackie standing a few feet away from the lean-to, still alert at his post.

Placing the pistol and knife behind his belt, Mac-Kenzie pulled on his moccasins and stepped from the shelter. A thick mist was rising from several creeks nearby, cloaking the trunks of the great pines in solemn whiteness. Such concealment for their campsite was not unwelcome at the present, but it still made John uneasy that they themselves could see so little of their surroundings.

With a word to Blackie he took his bow and strode silently into the fog-shrouded woods, soon disappearing among the ghostly trees as though he had never existed. The seaman took a seat close by the lean-to, watching over the sleeping girl and calmly awaiting the frontiersman's return. He kept all his weapons ready at hand.

John moved around the camp in a wide circle, his soft moccasins letting him feel and avoid putting his weight down on any branches or dry twigs which might break and announce his presence. He paused frequently to listen and peer into the milky silence around him.

When he had completed his circuit and was satisfied to have found no sign of other humans in the vicinity, he returned to camp. Becky was up now, quietly occupying herself with laying a fire for their morning meal.

Blackie stood as MacKenzie hung his bow on a corner of the lean-to. "You saw nothing?"

"Nothing. It appears we are alone for the moment. Yet after we've eaten I mean to have another look around. By then the mists will be risin', and I'll be better able to search the ground for tracks or other signs."

"It seems odd," Becky said, "that in all this vast wilderness our way should so quickly cross that of another. I would have thought one could journey for days in this country without meeting any human soul." She was cutting slices of venison into an iron spider, where a few rashers of bacon had already begun to simmer.

"'Tis not so strange when you give a thought to it," John answered. "The rivers and creeks are the natural highways o' this land, and are much used by the natives as well as those of our own kind who may chance to be travelin' through. As vast as this wilderness is," he added, laying another stick on the fire, "it is never so simple to lose oneself in it as is often imagined."

"But how might that be, lad?" Blackie asked. "It would seem this country is as wide and free as any great ocean — and almost as trackless."

"Aye. But you know that the oceans o' the world have their oft-traveled routes as well. And even those ships that may sail far from the lanes o' commerce must call at a port from time to time. The posts o' traders in the wilderness are much like ports o' call to a seafarer. It is a rare wanderer who will not put in at one of them soon or late, in search o' provisions, news, or human company." He reached out with his knife and took a venison steak from the pan, holding it before him to cool in the morning air.

"Talk is highly prized by lonely men, who have so very little of it. And there is talk at the tradin' posts o' many things: game, the weather, the mood o' the natives, the doin's o' the outside world, and o' course, other travelers in the back country. Such posts may be few in the Floridas, and distant one from the other, but still there is very little that happens in this land which is not known to all within a fortnight."

10

JACK THATCHER WATCHED the hulking back of Jacob LeBeau as the big half-breed bent to duck under the moss-draped limb of a thick live oak a short distance ahead, scarcely slowing his horse for the passage. Whatever else Thatcher might think of the man, there was no doubt that LeBeau was a skilled tracker. And he was proving to be a relentlessly persistent hunter as well

It had taken the frontiersman almost no time to find the place where MacKenzie and the others had crossed the city wall, and after only a few minutes of examining the ground he'd been able to reconstruct the entire sequence of events that had occurred the night before, describing them in economical detail to the small band of pursuers who accompanied him. Before noon they were already riding north, following the tracks of the fugitives on their way toward the St. Johns River.

Nor did the half-breed seem inclined to waste any more time than necessary bringing the chase to a conclusion. He had set a pace through the trees and dense undergrowth west of San Sebastian Creek that the city-bred riders in Tyrone's pay were having difficulty matching.

The day was hot, and even on the shaded forest trail the sweat ran freely from under their hats and down their collars, making dark stains on the backs of their shirts and beneath their armpits. Whether LeBeau liked it or not, Thatcher thought grimly, they must stop soon to rest the horses, if not themselves.

Some minutes later the big man in the lead drew rein at the edge of a small clearing. He turned his mount sideways on the trail and held up a hand as a warning.

"Wait here," he said. "All of you but the Indian. He can come forward, but only on foot. I've found where the three of 'em camped for the night."

Gratefully, Thatcher pulled up in the shade of a huge elm and slid from his saddle to the ground. Leaning against the side of his black stallion, he uncorked his water bottle and took a long delicious draught as the other men came alongside and dismounted.

The Indian advanced to join LeBeau at the edge of the clearing, while Simms and Ben Pike led their horses to a patch of grass some dozen yards away, picketing them in silence. It had been a hard ride so far, and no one felt much inclined toward conversation.

Pike found a comfortable spot beside a pine tree and sat down, stretching his legs out on the cushion of needles in front of him. His thin hatchet face showed no expression as he took a drink from his water bottle. Then he shifted his long poniard to a more comfortable position, pulled his slouch hat forward, and closed his eyes.

Bill Simms seemed unusually restless in the forest stillness. He paced back and forth beside the trail for several minutes after dismounting, flexing his broad shoulders and thick arms to work out the kinks from his ride. At last he straddled a fallen log and took out his hunting knife, occupying himself with carving deep gashes into the wood before him.

Thatcher watched his companions thoughtfully, glancing from time to time toward the clearing where LeBeau and the native were busy examining the signs of MacKenzie's camp.

The matter of the tracker's "final payment" after they had located their quarry was still a serious area of concern for him. There was no question about whether Tyrone's instructions would be carried out. Dread Jamie was not a man one disobeyed lightly. Nor could they afford any outside witnesses to what was planned for the frontiersman and his companions in the back country in any case.

The problem lay in exactly how the "payment" was to be made. Thatcher had an idea LeBeau was the kind of man who might take a lot of killing, and one who was unlikely to let his guard down even for a second in the wilderness. As he had no intention of facing the big half-breed alone in open combat, his companions would have to be let in on the plan at some point. Their aid would be needed in order to accomplish the deed with minimal risk.

But not too soon, Thatcher realized. None of the others could safely be trusted with that sort of secret for long. Simms was all brawn, with little brain to go with it. It would be almost impossible for him to hide their intentions from a canny man like LeBeau. Pike, on the other hand, was tight-lipped enough, and devious, but he took too great a pleasure in killing for its own sake. Not overly inclined to patience, the knife-fighter might choose to strike at the first opportunity which presented itself. And that opportunity could well come before they were fully certain of their quarry.

The native . . . ? He was possibly the best of them all in a fight, but notional like all redskins. It was hard to know what he might think of the plan. Best not to tell him anything until the moment was at hand.

Thatcher took another swallow of water and replaced the stopper with a sharp smack of his hand. The business was going to take some more thought, any way he looked at it. Perhaps the days ahead would suggest something . . . .

When he glanced up LeBeau was beckoning them toward the clearing. With a word to the others, Thatcher took hold of his stallion's reins and led the big horse forward along the trail.

They camped here," the frontiersman said, "cooked, spent one day, part of a night I think. Two men, one woman. Arrived with a horse, but did not leave with it." He shrugged. "Rain washed out some of the sign. Come."

Following the big man to the creek and along it for perhaps a mile to its mouth, they halted again and LeBeau looked over the area for several minutes. Finally he strode to the bank and knelt beside a small clump of brush at the water's edge.

"A boat," he said after a moment. "A boat and supplies, I'll wager. How they came by 'em is your guess." He rose and looked at the men behind him. "They're across the river now, maybe far into the wilderness. There's at least a dozen routes by water alone that they might have taken."

Thatcher was not entirely surprised, but the information was annoying nonetheless. "What," he asked the other man, "do you suggest we do?"

"Depends. We could call on the nearby plantations, find out where they got the boat, see if anything was said about a destination, or if anybody saw them cross." The big man frowned. "Not likely, though." He shook his head. "MacKenzie's too canny for that. We might split up . . ."

"No." Thatcher's voice was firm. "We will remain together, come what may. Those are Tyrone's orders. And it will give us the best chance of success when we do find them." There was, of course, another reason for keeping the party together, but the tall man said nothing of that.

LeBeau looked at Thatcher through narrowed eyes. "Well, perhaps if you'd some idea of their destination . . ."

Tyrone's man shrugged, avoiding the other's gaze. "Not for a certainty," he said after the barest hesitation. "But westward more than likely. There are too many settlements along the St. Marys to the north, and south would take them away from the Georgia colony where they could hope to reach safety."

"Westward." LeBeau paused in thought. "That still leaves several routes, by both water and land. But most of them tend to come together after a time." He thought a minute longer, then nodded.

"All right. We're mounted and they are not. When they leave whatever waterway they've taken they must travel on foot. If we cross with our horses tonight, in a few days — with luck — we will be ahead of them. I know all the white men in that country, and many of the natives." He smiled. "There are few secrets on the frontier and we will learn of their passing sooner or later. If we can arrange to be waiting for them . . ."

He glanced at Thatcher, who nodded his agreement. Mounting quickly, they set off at a trot along the forest trail, southward toward Picolata and the crossing of the St. Johns.

MacKenzie wiped the grease from his knife and sheathed it, then rose from the breakfast fire and looked around him. By now the fog was above the lower branches of the trees and it was rapidly becoming thinner.

"I'll have that bit of a look around now," he said. "Do you both pack for our journey and douse the fire in the meanwhile. I'll be wantin' to leave this place straightway upon my return."

He took his quiver and water bottle from the lean-to, picked up his bow and started away from camp. Before he had taken a dozen steps, they all heard a deep voice calling to them from the surrounding trees:

"Hello the fire! Is it all right for a man to come in?"

John glanced quickly back at his companions without moving from where he stood. Becky was kneeling by the fire, calmly picking up her knife as if to slice more venison for the skillet. The sailor quietly took his pistol from his belt and placed it in his lap, then covered it with the folds of his long pea-jacket. He glanced up at Mac-Kenzie and nodded.

"Are you by yourself?" John moved a few feet to his left as he spoke. He stopped beside the trunk of one of the big pine trees, standing partly behind it.

"Aye. I'm alone, and I'm friendly. Just lookin' for a

drop o' somethin' warm to drink, an' perhaps a bite to eat if you've got it to spare. Maybe a little conversation too."

"Come in, then. But do you move slowly and keep your hands where we can see them."

A large man stepped forward from the trees, leading a roan horse. He was a Negro, dressed in light buckskins that were almost new. A pistol and knife were in his belt, and he carried a long rifle cradled in his right arm. A quick glance at the man's size and his leather boots told John that this could not be the same man whose tracks he had seen the night before.

After tying his horse to a nearby bush, the newcomer approached the fire with an easy tread. "Jeremiah's the name," he said cheerfully, reaching down with his left hand to take the cup Becky offered him. "Only Jeremiah. No family name, for I never had no real family to speak of." He took a swallow of tea, then glanced at those around the fire.

John nodded. "John MacKenzie." He indicated his companions. "Mr. Robert Teague, and Miss Becky Campbell." He saw no reason to volunteer any further information to the stranger at present.

"Pleased to know you." The black man's eyes rested thoughtfully on each of them for a brief moment, but he made no other comment as he squatted before the fire and took another swallow of tea. He laid his rifle beside him on the ground within easy reach, apparently from long habit.

"Travelin' far?" the visitor asked casually as Becky placed a cut of venison in the skillet and added fresh wood to the fire. His manner was relaxed and agreeable.

"Here and there." John shrugged. "As the road takes us." His eyes narrowed slightly. "Yourself?"

"The same." The black man glanced up at the frontiersman, then reached out to pour himself more tea. "I'm a hunter by trade. I go where the game leads me."

Blackie replaced the pistol in his belt, then rose from the ground and stretched lazily. He took a few steps to his right around the fire. "What sort o' game might that be?" he asked conversationally. "From your outfit you seem to be travelin' a bit light for a long hunter, if I might say so."

The sailor was now standing on the opposite side of the newcomer from John, with Becky to one side out of any potential line of fire. MacKenzie thought he saw this fact register in the Negro's eyes, but the man gave no other sign that he was aware of his new position.

"Why," Jeremiah answered calmly, leaning back on his left elbow, "I hunt that game which'll bring me the most profit, always. I'm a man who means to make his fortune in this frontier land. But since I've poor family connections, as you might say, and nothin' at all in the way of an inheritance, I do whatever I can if it pays well enough." He glanced at Blackie out of the corners of his eyes. "At the moment," he went on, "that happens to be bringin' back runaway slaves."

There was an uncomfortable silence, although John

found himself not entirely surprised by the news. He had suspected as much when this well-armed newcomer appeared in the forest so shortly after that other, unknown man had left his bare footprints nearby.

Better than anyone here, John knew that on the frontier each man's business was his own — especially when it was a legal one. Still he'd never had much stomach for trafficking in men's souls, though from childhood he'd heard all the arguments in favor of the institution. It occurred to him that perhaps his present distaste was increased by the fact that here was a black man who sought to profit from the bondage of his own kind.

But it was none of their affair, and MacKenzie carefully kept his expression neutral while glancing at his companions. Blackie's face was mild too, though the seaman no longer seemed to meet the slave-hunter's eyes directly. However, Becky's feelings were readily apparent, and the girl could not keep them entirely to herself.

"It would seem," she said quietly, in a voice turned icy cold, "that there might be other ways for a man to make his fortune. Ways that do not require the misery of others to provide for his own advancement!"

Jeremiah looked at her sharply, then turned his head and gazed into the fire. He said nothing for a long moment.

"Ma'am," he replied finally, sitting up and laying his cup on the ground beside him, "I take no special pride in how I make my livin'. But as things stand I'll not apologize for it neither. I was given my freedom by my former master on his deathbed, and for that I'm grateful. But when I walked away from his plantation I'd nothin' in this world but the clothes on my back and the paper in my hand. What would I have done? Farm some other man's acres for a share that'd barely keep me alive? Work for the pitiful wages some strugglin' tradesman might pay?

"I never had no proper trade m'self but huntin' an' fightin'. There in North Georgia I'd hunted wolves an' painters in the wild country, fought time to time as my master had the need — Injuns, outlaws, even pirates now an' again. In Africa they say my people were Ashanti. Great warriors. So I reckon maybe it's in my blood.

"And I guess their pride is in my blood too, for I'm a man has the need to walk tall in this new land." He looked at the others around the campfire.

"I could see from when I was a child that the men who walked tallest in these colonies were always the men o' property. Men of means, men of affairs. There's a gentleman o' color a mite south and west of here owns a section o' land and twenty slaves to work it. He's a respected man, a proud man. And I reckon I'm just every bit the man he is.

"I got my code," Jeremiah went on. "I don't kill nobody I hunt 'less they force me to it, and I don't mistreat 'em. Only what's needed to bring 'em in. I do my job an' I earn my pay, an' that there's more than a lot can claim." He glanced from Becky to the sailor, then let his eyes rest on MacKenzie.

"And there's some things I wouldn't do for no amount o' money, neither. I won't do murder." He paused. "Not even for a hundred guineas!"

John's eyes fixed the slave-hunter coldly. It was several seconds before he spoke. "Do you happen to know, then," he asked carefully, "where a man might earn a hundred guineas for such a deed?"

"Aye. I do. And so will every other man on the frontier before this fortnight's out. Tyrone's made no secret o' the job he wants done." The black man met MacKenzie's eyes. "He wants you dead, mister. And the rest of you too I think — or worse."

There was a minute of silence. Jeremiah shrugged and poured himself more tea.

"I never give it a thought m'self," he said. "Even before I met up with you I'd a idea earnin' that money might take a bit o' doin'. Collectin' it from Tyrone might take a bit o' doin' too, when you come right down to it. So even if I was o' the mind, which I'm not, 'twouldn't be worth the roll o' the dice to me. Not with my own blood bein' the stakes, as you might say." He looked at the three of them.

"'Specially," he added, "when there's others hereabouts who seem to have a deal more interest in the job than what I've got."

11 🌿

"OTHERS?" JOHN LOOKED HARD at the slave-hunter. "What others?"

"There's five of 'em in all. Four o' Tyrone's men, includin' that Injun he's got in his pay, and one other. Big half-breed name o' LeBeau. Meaner than a gator with the toothache, so I hear tell. All of 'em are well mounted. They crossed the river last night at Picolata 'bout a half hour after I did."

Jeremiah took the plate of food Becky handed him.

"Thank you kindly, miss," he said with a smile. "It's always a pleasure not havin' to make do with my own catchin' and cookin'." He cut a piece of meat and placed it in his mouth with his knife point. Then he looked at John.

"I watched 'em along for a bit. Knew that was a rough outfit right off, an' I'd no wish to cross trails with 'em accidental-like if I could manage not to. So I followed 'em down the Path to Alachua four or five miles till they made a late camp, then came on up thisaway. Figured north was most likely where I'd find that fella I been huntin' anyhow. And me, I like travelin' by moonlight."

He cut another bite of meat and then fell silent, giving his full attention to the food on his plate while John considered what this news meant for himself and his two companions.

Some of Tyrone's pursuers might be unfamiliar with the frontier, but even so they were sure to be tough, hard men. The native would be in his element of course, and all the more dangerous because of it. LeBeau .

MacKenzie knew the man by reputation, and had seen him in passing a time or two at travelers' stops in the wilderness. Nothing of what he knew was good. LeBeau was a brute with the strength and fierceness of one of those huge bears of the western lands, and with even fewer moral scruples. But he was cunning and clever for all of that, and he knew the Florida back country as well or better than any white man in it, MacKenzie included.

With such men on their trail John and his companions would be in constant danger now. News of strangers in the wilderness traveled quickly, and they would have to keep out of sight as much as possible, always avoiding known paths and settlements.

Yet that promised to be easier said than done. For the land was crisscrossed with well-marked trails, many in regular use long before the coming of the white man. On the rivers canoe traffic was frequent, and there were many native villages located near these waterways.

It meant a difficult journey at best, and to make matters worse, as they neared their destination this roundabout means of travel would become impossible. The west coast of Florida was ringed with dense swamps for miles inland. The natives might know of trails and hidden water routes through them, but John did not. He knew of no sure way to reach that island in the Gulf except by river.

A sudden thought brought his attention back to the slave-hunter beside the campfire. "Tyrone's men. You say they were camped upon the Path to Alachua?" he asked.

"Aye." Jeremiah wiped grease from his plate with a piece of johnnycake and placed it in his mouth. "Saw 'em bed down some four or five miles along it. Left 'em there around midnight."

"'Twas clearly too dark to scout sign when they crossed the St. Johns — yet they did not wait, but came inland straightway?"

The black man set his empty plate on the ground

and reached for the pot of tea. "Didn't seem much inclined to scout sign, to my way o' thinking. They rode hard, like they knew where they was going. And like they didn't mean to waste around any gettin' there."

MacKenzie nodded thoughtfully. This put a slightly different complexion on the matter. "They were all well mounted, you say?"

As well as I've seen in this country." The slave-hunter smiled. "I'd give a pretty for that big black the tall thin one was ridin'."

It seemed the pursuers did not intend to follow their trail directly then, but perhaps meant to intercept them at some point farther west. If John and his friends were to keep well north of the Path to Alachua they might avoid detection until they reached the San Juanito or the Santa Fe River. And if they could evade Tyrone's men that far . . .

But there was another question to be considered here.

How was it, MacKenzie asked himself, that their enemies could plan to intercept them at all, if they'd no idea of their destination? The most logical routes of escape would be to the north or the northwest. Yet the followers had ridden due west, and without hesitating even briefly.

He looked curiously at Blackie across the clearing, wondering just how many others might know the "secret" of the treasure at the mouth of the San Juanito River. The sailor was busy packing supplies for the journey, and seemed unaware of John's gaze. MacKenzie decided he would say nothing of this for the time being. But it was something to be remembered.

He stooped to pick up his pack and weapons, glancing at the black man who still sat cross-legged beside the remains of their fire. "Under the circumstances," he said, straightening and meeting the visitor's eyes, "you'll forgive us if we tarry here no longer in conversation. We'd best be on our way. For there are some miles to cover before our next night's rest." John paused and continued mildly, "I would consider it a favor if you were to forget about this chance meeting, should you come upon any others along the trail."

"No need to worry on that account," Jeremiah answered seriously. "I've no wish to meet up with any o' that crowd, now or later. I never had no dealin's with Tyrone, and I don't want any with his kind."

Becky had shouldered her pack and approached the fire, halting before the slave-hunter. She spoke quietly.

"I cannot truly say I'm sorry for my words earlier, though I'll confess I may understand your reasons a bit better now. But I must still believe that there are more honorable ways to gain what you seek. I have no answers, yet I will pray upon the matter to Providence." She paused, then added, "And I hope that you may too."

The black man looked up at her for a moment, then lowered his eyes. "I might do that, Miss, though I've little enough experience at it. I'll think on the matter at any rate." He handed her his cup and turned back toward the fire. "You keep well, y'hear? The three o' you."

John glanced at Blackie, who stood ready beside him, then reached out and placed a hand on the girl's shoulder. "It's time," he said. "You keep well yourself, Jeremiah."

With a wave to the slave-hunter he turned away and strode from the clearing, the others following behind. In minutes they were out of sight of the camp and its lone visitor.

The hours and miles dissolved behind them, lost in an endless expanse of dense forests and broad meadows, of gently rolling hills and shining spring-fed creeks. They were well into the sandhill country now, that low spine of uplands running the length of the Florida peninsula from Apalachee in the north to the great lake and river of the ancient Calusa some four hundred miles to the south.

There was little undergrowth among the tall pines, so the walking was easy enough, though John was still taking care to avoid the most-traveled routes. From time to time they passed broad swamplands, crisscrossed by shallow sloughs and domed over with the pale green tops of the stately bald cypress. At other times they skirted hardwood hammocks thick with blackgum, oak, hickory, elm and magnolia.

Birds in rampant profusion filled the air with their

noise and color and movement. Sparrows, woodpeckers, egrets, hawks and soaring cranes feasted on legions of swarming insects and other small denizens of the forest, as well as on the diverse fruits of the lush foliage. Everywhere the travelers found themselves in the midst of full and vibrant life, the age-old cycles of birth, mating, death; of hunter and hunted.

The larger woodland creatures were more cautious than their feathered compatriots, wisely choosing to stay out of sight of both prey and predator alike. Yet their sign was everywhere if one knew how to see it. At the noonings John pointed out the tracks and droppings of raccoon, opossum, deer, bear, wild turkey and a multitude of others including many serpents and lizards. Once they saw the tracks of a stalking panther, no more than an hour old.

"You must learn to see everything that is about you," he told his companions as they walked. "Knowledge of what is here will give you sustenance in the wild, and it is your best protection against danger as well. A serpent may as easily drop from the limb above your head as be found sleepin' upon the log at your feet."

They saw that the frontiersman's own eyes were constantly moving as they traveled, from the ground to the branches of the trees to the distant horizon and back again. In time they began to form the same habit. The woodlands and prairies were never barren of life, even at those quiet times of morning, afternoon or night when all about them seemed to be sleeping.

During the next two days Blackie and Becky learned much of the Florida wilderness, though it was clear to them as well as John that they had far more left to learn in this land of endless diversity. To discover all that was here might easily take several lifetimes.

MacKenzie was encouraged by their progress however. It was a stern country they journeyed through, as filled with danger as it was with life and beauty. He could not be constantly watching over his friends; so they must learn to recognize at least some of its hazards for themselves.

Early on the second morning they came upon a brown bear stretching high to place its claw marks on the bole of a tree. At John's silent signal the three halted where they were, simply watching while the animal finished staking its territorial claim. Still standing upright, it turned and regarded the humans for several minutes. Then it shook its head, as though thoroughly disgusted by this collection of unwanted tourists, and dropped to all fours to amble slowly off into the forest.

As they proceeded on their way, Becky commented on the creature's apparent indifference. "He seemed to care not at all that we were here in his land," she said. "I would have thought he'd have been more curious."

"He was curious enough," John said, "but he was not foolish. The bear watched to see only whether or not we presented a danger to him. When it was clear that we did not, he chose to leave us alone. It is a lesson men might learn, for it is often the wisest course.

"Had we approached or made a threatening sound," he went on, "'twould have been a different matter entirely. If the creature sensed harm he would not have hesitated to attack, with the result that he, and perhaps we, might now be dead. We merely watched also, cautiously as he did. Then all chose the course of prudence: to live, and to let live."

John looked at his companions. "Needless killin' is seldom the way o' the beasts in the wild, as it should not be with us. For food, yes, for our sustenance and our survival. To protect ourselves from danger, by all means. But no one save a fool will take another life lightly, whether it be that of a wild animal or of another human bein'."

For several minutes they walked in silence. Then MacKenzie added thoughtfully, "The matter is not always so simple, you understand. There are some creatures that will perceive danger where none is there, and so will attack without seemin' provocation. Others, like the weasel among chickens, will indeed kill wantonly and repeatedly once the fever of blood is upon them. It is best never to trust too far to what we may perceive as an animal's better nature."

He paused, then added quietly: "I have discovered that there are some men, as well as beasts, in these categories as well."

On the second night they camped in a thick stand of pine among vast expanses of saw palmetto and wax myrtle bushes. They had been traveling through such country for the better part of the day, following a narrow Indian trail southward toward the river the Spaniards called the Santa Fe.

John had cautioned his friends earlier to be wary of rattlesnakes in this country, for the poisonous creatures were known to be especially partial to the thick palmetto brakes that surrounded them now on every side. When their shelter was raised and the fire made, he took a fresh hemp rope from his pack and laid it in a careful circle around the lean-to.

"'Twill not always keep the serpents outside," he told his companions, "but they've tender bellies and do not care much for crossin' the sharp bristles. At least 'tis better than no protection at all."

With his bow he'd killed several birds during the day's trek, and these were soon spitted on palmetto spears to roast over the coals. It was almost an hour till sundown, for MacKenzie preferred to camp early and leave no fire burning after dark which might guide others to their resting place.

They'd been uncommonly fortunate so far, and had seen no one at all along the way, neither Indians nor white men. It would not surprise John if they had been observed from time to time by a hunting native. But his hope was that the fact would not be reported beyond the local village of such a chance observer, at least for the time being.

Still, they could not have such luck forever. The

woods they were passing through now were so thick that no traveler could hope to avoid trails entirely, even though the ones MacKenzie chose were not the most commonly used. Speed was their best ally, and he had pushed his companions hard to cover the sixty miles that lay between their first camp in the wilderness and his planned destination on the Santa Fe River. He estimated it would take another day and a half of steady walking to bring them to that place.

When they had finished eating, the shadows were already swallowing up the contours of the dense forest around them. Frogs and crickets were engaged in their nightly serenade, and an owl's hunting cry broke the evening stillness not very many yards away.

John was tired, but he'd deliberately volunteered for the first watch. Blackie needed the rest more than he did, and he could stretch his time to give the older man an extra hour or so of sleep before there was any need to wake him.

The sailor and the girl were making their beds in the gathering twilight as MacKenzie knelt to scatter the fire. Suddenly he froze, listening. There had been a sound on the trail a short distance away which did not seem to be native to the forest.

A minute later he heard low voices: ". . . been smellin' that smoke for the last half hour. It's somewheres near, Jamie. Right close to the trail, I'll wager."

"I c'n smell it too now, Reet. I wonder if'n . . ."

"Hush!"

Both men fell silent and MacKenzie knew they had seen a faint glow from the coals, or perhaps some other sign of their camp. He rose and stepped to the edge of the tiny clearing, partly hidden among a stand of small cedars. At the same time he caught Blackie's eye. The sailor had heard too, and was already moving away from the fire into the shadows with Becky close behind him.

They waited for several minutes, but there was no hailing call. That in itself signaled danger, for no one of peaceful intent ever approached a camp in the wilderness unannounced. It was a strictly observed rule borne of the need for self-preservation more than of courtesy. All men on the frontier went armed, and most were not slow to shoot.

With the large knife in his left hand John strained his ears into the gathering night. He heard nothing now but the frogs and crickets. He considered backing into the woods behind him to scout the area, but decided it was safer to wait where he was for the time being.

Suddenly and unexpectedly, Blackie and the girl stepped from their hiding place into the open. A moment later John saw the reason.

At the edge of the trees behind them stood a lean, rangy young man in dirty buckskins. He held two pistols leveled at the man and woman, the hammers of both pulled back and ready to fire.

"Looky here what I found, Reet!" The young man was grinning broadly. "You bring that jug along and I reckon we c'n just have us a party!"

12 ✹

THERE WAS A BRIEF SILENCE. Then the second man spoke from the darkness a few yards off. "How many'd you catch, Jamie boy?"

"Two. One's a mangy ol' piece o' crow bait I'll purely hate to waste powder an' ball on. But t'other's right fetchin'. *Right* fetchin'. Come on in, Reet, an' I'll match you for who gets the first dance!"

"Shut up that ugly yap o' yours an' look sharp, boy! I'll swear I seen the tracks o' *three* back yonder. Might be another right close by!" The voice in the darkness came from a different place this time. The hidden man was moving about so that no one could get a bearing on his location from the sound.

"Aw, Reet. You know you can't rightly read good sign in this grass an' leaves an' all. Ain't seen a proper track the livelong day. C'mon in an' let's have us a drink!"

There was no answer from the man in the thicket. John glanced at the one called Jamie and saw uncertainty growing on his grimy face. His pistols still held steady on the sailor and the girl, but his eyes had begun to wander to the shadows outside the campfire's glow.

When they rested briefly on another section of woods, MacKenzie took the opportunity to ease himself back a few feet into deeper shadow. Kneeling there, he silently drew his pistol, but did not dare cock it. To risk even that small sound might give these men a deadly advantage. And he had no idea where the one called Reet was at this moment.

Suddenly there was a faint rustle of leaves and a darker shadow loomed over John, no more than three feet away. There wasn't time to think, for in another second the man would be upon him.

Drawing the hammer of his pistol back with his left hand and squeezing the trigger at the same time, MacKenzie thrust the muzzle up hard into the other man's belly and released the hammer. The flash and hiss of the priming load preceded the explosion by the briefest instant, but it was all the warning Reet ever got.

The half-inch ball tore through his vitals with murderous force, pushing him two steps backward before he lost his footing and crashed heavily into a nearby stand of saw palmettos. He lay on the crumpled fans moaning softly, knowing with shocked realization that he would never see another dawn.

At the instant the charge went off John threw himself sideways, rolling over twice and coming to his knees in the darkness a good eight feet from where he'd been kneeling. He turned and looked quickly toward the clearing.

Jamie was no longer in sight. In his place Blackie stood with his feet apart, peering into the shadows of the forest. In the sailor's hands John saw both of the younger man's pistols. One of them was smoking faintly. The barrel of the second was stained with a patch of fresh blood, glowing redly in what remained of their fire's light. Becky was kneeling nearby, apparently unharmed. She also was gazing into the dark woods.

When MacKenzie appeared at the edge of the clearing the seaman glanced at him, then seemed to relax slightly.

"Not as much fight in that lad as I might a' thought, once push come to shove," he said, shaking his head. "Made 'em a hair tougher in my day, I think." He thrust the empty pistol into his belt and stooped to wipe the bloody barrel of the other on the grass at his feet. John was already reloading his own weapon as he moved to the center of the clearing.

"Sorry to let him get away like that," the sailor said, rising, "but at least he'll have a sore skull for a day or two." He grinned. "—And maybe not so much of a hankerin' after womenfolks for a while now, neither!"

John took a step toward Becky. "Are you all right?" he asked.

"I'm fine, thanks to Blackie here. I might have thought to help him, but it's little enough chance he gave me. Before I could fairly see what he was about, it was over."

"When I saw the flash o' your pistol in the darkness I knew 'twas no time to be wastin' about," the seaman responded. "This fellow looked over to see what was happenin', and I did what it was in my mind to do all along. —And besides . . ." He looked at the girl out of the corners of his eyes. ". . . it may be I needed to save the lad from a worser fate in any case. I'd already seen from the lady's eyes what she might a' done to him, given the chance."

Becky blushed slightly, then shook her head. "You give me too much credit," she said. "I'd have done only what I had to do, no more."

"'Twould a' been enough, I'm bettin'." Blackie looked at John. "That's a lass for a fightin' man, lad, and no mistake. Cool as you please the whole time. No tears, no frettin', not even a word. An' thinkin'. I could see that clear enough. Thinkin' all the while o' what needed to be done."

John looked at the sailor, and then at the girl. She did not meet his eyes.

"I'd best be takin' care o' what's out there," he said after a moment, indicating with a toss of his head the palmetto brake where Reet's body lay. "Then we must all try to get some rest. I'd prefer to move our camp after this, but it's too risky now in the darkness — and with one o' them still about perhaps. We'll just have to keep a good watch tonight, and hope for the best."

When MacKenzie reached the spot, Reet was dead. John took the man's weapons, then dragged the body a short distance to the sandy bank of a dry creek bed where he caved in loose earth around it to make a rough grave. It was little enough to do, but on balance John had few regrets. He'd no intention of risking his life digging a proper grave for a man like this, one who'd chosen to live his life like an animal among men.

The trading post was a simple one-room log cabin, no more than thirty feet long by half that wide. At one end a rough table and bench stood before a clay hearth, cold now in the late spring evening. At the other end was a counter made of heavy wood planks laid across two barrels. Behind that and around the walls of the low room a jumbled assortment of boxes, barrels and loose trade goods rested on the dirt floor, stacked randomly and with no apparent attempt at organization.

The shutters were closed now to ward off mosquitoes and other night visitors, and a smoky oil lamp provided additional defense against the bothersome "swamp angels." Jack Thatcher found the atmosphere close and oppressive, the more so since the presence of himself and three other big men seemed to fill the small place to overflowing.

LeBeau and Bill Simms were two of the men. The fourth was a burly Irish trader with greasy auburn hair and a pale scar beneath his left eye. He was dressed in faded woolen breeches and a soiled buckskin shirt open at the collar. At the moment he was pouring whiskey from a clay jug into several tin cups on the counter.

"MacKenzie." The trader handed a cup to Simms. "I know him. But I've not seen him for some months now." He paused and seemed to think. "Late last fall, I'd guess it was."

After handing a second cup to Thatcher, the Irishman hesitated, regarding LeBeau's straight black hair and high cheekbones for a long minute. Then he shrugged and pushed a cup across the counter to the half-breed before pouring another drink for himself.

"A solitary man, MacKenzie," the trader observed casually, his eyes on his visitors. "Always seems to travel alone and keeps his own counsel. What is it you might be wantin' of him?"

"He's not travelin' alone this time," LeBeau said, throwing back his head and downing his drink in one gulp. "He's abroad with another man. And a woman." He placed his cup back on the counter.

"A woman, y'say?" The redhead moved the jug slightly nearer to the big half-breed but did not offer to pour again. "Injun woman?"

"White woman. Heard they was all headin' westward together, maybe travelin' on the rivers."

"Could be." The Irishman shrugged. "I've heard nothin' about it myself, though." He finished his drink and reached for the jug. LeBeau's hand got to it first.

"Speakin' o' women," the tracker said slowly, pulling the clay vessel toward him, "where's that squaw woman o' yours right now?" He lifted the jug to his shoulder. "Might be we'll need to wait here awhile, till after we've got some word of MacKenzie and his party." He took a long pull, his eyes never leaving the trader. "Might be a right long wait." He set the jug down with a thump.

Something akin to fear flickered suddenly in the Irishman's eyes. He glanced at Thatcher and Bill Simms, but found nothing there to encourage him. "She's about," he said. "Here and about." He took the jug from where LeBeau had put it and poured himself a large drink, downing it quickly

The big half-breed said nothing. He leaned heavily on the counter and watched the trader through hooded eyes. Thatcher glanced at Simms, started to speak, but thought better of it. There was an awkward silence.

Suddenly Thatcher found his attention drawn to a sound outside the cabin. It was a sound of running feet, and had been nagging at his subconscious for several seconds before he became fully aware of it. He turned to face the door, his hand dropping to the pistol in his belt Simms turned with him.

A moment later the door burst open, banging sharply against the wall on its leather hinges. A lean young man stood framed in the opening, wild-eyed and breathless. His hair was matted with blood and his buckskins were torn and stained with dirt and grass. He glanced quickly at the men in the room, then stumbled to the bar.

"Lemme have a drink o' that, trader! I been needin' some o' that ever since last night 'bout this time!" He took the jug over his shoulder and drank for a long while, finally setting the whiskey back on the counter and wiping his mouth with the back of his hand. It was another minute before he could find his breath to speak. At last he shook his head and looked at the others as if seeing them for the first time.

"They done kilt Reet," he said to nobody in particular. "Kilt him deader 'n a post. That big 'un gut-shot him, sure as I'm standin' here. I seen it happen, an' then the little 'un got my guns from me somehow an' laid me up 'side the head. Reckon I was lucky to get out'n there with my scalp!"

The young man named Jamie looked from Thatcher to Simms and then back to the trader. When nobody said anything he picked up the jug and drank again. After that he turned his back to the bar, leaning heavily against it on both elbows.

"Got lost in that dang swampland out there, all night an' half the day I reckon. Found the trail to this place 'most by chance." He paused, then shrugged. "Reet an' me, we's from up Georgia way, up on the Saltilla. Don't

155

know this here country worth a damn!"

Thatcher was watching the young man curiously. After a moment he asked, "The two men you came upon? Was there a woman with them, by any chance?"

Jamie looked quickly at the taller man, then avoided his eyes. "Uh-huh, there was a woman. Young woman. Right pretty, too."

Except for a brief glance over his shoulder when the door first opened, LeBeau had remained with his back to the others throughout the conversation. Now he turned around.

"The larger man?" he asked, meeting the newcomer's eyes for the first time. "A frontiersman, would you say? Dressed in buckskins?"

Jamie shrugged. "Didn't see very much o' that one, tell you the truth. He was skulkin' around out in the dark. That's how come he managed to shoot Reet, from ambush, like."

"The other one?" Thatcher had taken a step closer. "A shorter man, maybe five foot six? Older, with sandy hair? Maybe wearing a stocking cap on his head?"

"That's him all right!" Jamie raised a hand and touched his matted scalp tenderly. "Reckon I won't forget that feller any time soon, not with what-all he gave me!"

Thatcher nodded, then looked at LeBeau. "What do you think?" he asked. "Two men and a woman, one of them a dead ringer for that ol' sea-dog. And there's few enough others likely to be abroad in that part o' the country."

The big tracker met his eyes. "Aye," he said slowly.

"It's him all right. It's MacKenzie."

Thatcher indicated the door with a jerk of his head. "Then we had best be on our way now," he said shortly. "'Tis moonlight out, and with a few hours' hard riding we can be near to where they were seen. By day, with luck, you will be able to pick up their trail."

LeBeau nodded, then turned to the young man beside him. "You will tell me where you were when first you came upon those three," he said, lowering his thick brows. "You will tell me how you traveled from the time you left Georgia until you met them. I know all the routes, and when you have told me I will know where to find their trail." He paused, watching closely for Jamie's reply.

The young man looked from LeBeau to Thatcher and then back again. A sly grin crept slowly across his youthful features. He had followed the conversation well enough, and knew that for some reason these men were hunting the strangers who'd killed his brother. He'd an idea they might exact the revenge he so dearly wished upon MacKenzie and his party, and the thought pleased him. Yet there was no reason why he should not also turn the situation to practical advantage. Without answering, he turned and picked up the jug from the counter.

"Well, now," he said carefully, hefting the liquor to his shoulder, "I might be able to do that — an' then again I might not." He took a long pull, making the moment last. "Seems to me," he went on, replacing the jug on the bar, "that you-all want to find this feller an' his party pretty bad. That's your business, o' course. But then where I seen 'em out there is my business." He paused.

"Seems like to me we ought to be able to do some business together." Jamie lifted his eyes to the men around him. "Though it might take a small amount o' cash to like, grease the wheels, as they say."

Thatcher gazed thoughtfully into the young man's eyes. The information could be worth a few coins at that, though it was hardly in the tall man's nature to spend good money for what could be had by other means. And there was still the need for secrecy regarding MacKenzie's fate. A man who'd sell information to one, would as likely sell it to another.

"Now I like that." It was LeBeau who spoke. "It's a wily man who sees matters so clearly." Glancing at the half-breed, Thatcher was surprised to find that the big man was smiling — the first time in their association he could ever remember him doing so.

"We might do business at that," the tracker continued, laying a bearlike paw on Jamie's shoulder. "But you understand that all our goods are in the saddlebags of our horses out yonder. If you're in a mood to talk business, perhaps we should step outside for a bit."

If the young man had not already consumed more than a pint of the trader's moonshine, he might have wondered briefly at this big frontiersman's sudden change in attitude. As it was however, Jamie was conscious only of the warm glow of satisfaction at how cleverly he was turning the present matter to his advantage.

Reet had always treated him as a mental inferior, never trusting him to arrange even the simplest of affairs, and quick to criticize his best efforts. If his older brother could just see him now . . .

The two men stepped out into the night and Bill Simms turned to follow, but Thatcher stopped him with an impatient gesture. Closing the door, the tall man took Simms' arm and led him quietly back to the bar. The trader refilled their cups, and they drank without speaking.

Only once were their thoughts interrupted by a shrill scream, and that was cut off almost immediately. Then for a long time they heard nothing at all.

After a while LeBeau returned to the cabin, and soon afterward the three left together, quickly covering the distance to the grove some quarter of a mile away where Ben Pike and the Indian waited with their horses. In minutes they were all riding north in the moonlight, toward the natural bridge of the Santa Fe River and the scrub-covered hill country beyond it, where they would once more pick up their quarry's trail.

After the sounds of their hoofbeats had faded into the distance, a dark figure rose silently from the shadow of a woodpile at the back of the trading post. He glanced at the Indian girl beside him and nodded toward the open door of the cabin.

"Y'had best go to your man now," he said in a low voice. "He'll be wonderin' about you, and may be in need o' some small comfort this night, I'm thinkin'. My thanks for your help, and for the provisions from your kitchen." Jeremiah paused and laid a hand carefully on hers. "Y' needn't mention my callin' unless you're a mind to. It might only worry him the more."

He turned and walked across the clearing to where his horse stood concealed in the trees behind the cook-shack and the palmetto dwelling of the trader and his woman. Untying the reins, the slave-hunter placed his sack of provisions over the saddle and mounted. Then he pointed the roan's head to the north and began to walk his mount slowly through the moonlight after Tyrone's men.

If you had asked him, the black man could have given you no good reason for his decision to ride that way. He did not entirely understand himself why he felt a desire to help MacKenzie and his companions against the men who pursued them. Perhaps it was something in his warrior's blood. Perhaps it was something else.

He knew only that at the moment it seemed like the right thing to do.

13

A LITTLE BEFORE NOON on the fourth day, MacKenzie and his companions arrived at a low bluff overlooking the Santa Fe. The river was some fifty yards wide where it passed beneath them here, curving snakelike between thick stands of cypress overgrown with vines and Spanish moss. The water was colored almost black from the tannin of decaying plant matter, and by the movement of scattered leaves on the surface they could tell that at this place the dark current was swift and deep.

Below them and to their right was a level bank perhaps a dozen yards wide by as many deep, lushly carpeted with coarse grass but almost bare of all other growth. Downstream of this the shore sank several inches to a deeply shaded hollow, covered over with dead leaves and studded with gnarled cypress knees. Clearly this was an area which was often submerged during the flood season.

On a patch of sand a few yards back from where they stood and hidden from the river by the curve of the bluff, John built a small fire and they prepared a meal. The smoke would be dissipated by the trees overhead, and in daylight the fire itself was almost invisible.

To MacKenzie's knowledge there were no white men anywhere about except for a trader who had a post some dozen miles to the west and south, near the high spring and the point where the Santa Fe reappeared after passing underground for several miles. Nor was he aware of any Indian settlements any closer. But still it cost nothing to be cautious.

He did not wish to risk a fire after dark, so this might be the last cooked meal they ate for several days. Here John intended to build a raft that would take them the rest of the way to their destination by water.

MacKenzie knew it would be a chancy proposition at best. It was hardly likely they could complete the trip down the Santa Fe and San Juanito rivers without being observed at least by the natives, even though they would travel a good part of the distance by night. But he could think of no other way of bypassing the great swamps that still lay between them and the Gulf coast.

He was sure there were Indian settlements downstream on the San Juanito, although having no experience on that stretch of the river he could make no accurate guess as to their location. His hope was that by the time his party was seen and word had gotten back to their pursuers, they would already have arrived at the river's mouth.

The return trip was something else to be considered, especially if the quantity of gold and silver they were to transport came anywhere close to Blackie's glowing predictions. But MacKenzie decided he would cross that bridge when he came to it.

The Gulf was shallow along the coast, and if the weather was fair they might go north or south on the raft to another waterway, following that for some distance inland. Or perhaps Tyrone's men would abandon the chase, though John admitted he considered that unlikely. If given no other choice, they would simply have to fight their way back.

When they had eaten, Blackie and MacKenzie set to work felling young trees for the raft. It was hard work, and the afternoon sun was hot in the little clearing beside the river. But with everyone's help, the construction was nearly finished by the time day began its slow decline into twilight.

It was not a pretty craft, but it was sturdy and roomy, some fifteen feet long by six wide. It had been lashed together tightly with lianas and what rope they had brought with them. A small shelter of palmetto thatch had been built at one end, and Blackie had managed to rig a mast so they could use the tarpaulin for a sail if the wind happened to favor them.

While the sailor and the girl erected the lean-to and laid out their bedrolls, John stripped the branches from several slender trees with his knife as a more certain means of propulsion. Laying these poles beside the raft on the grassy strand, he stepped back to view their preparations. Satisfied at last that they had done all they could with what was available, he began to climb the sandy hillock back to their camp.

Stars were already appearing in the sky and the moon was up, three-quarters full. John was tired, but he felt no immediate desire for sleep. He found a place beneath a huge elm at the edge of the bluff and sat there with his arms across his knees, gazing out over the dark water.

Silver ripples danced on the river among the deeper shadows of moss-laden trees. Crickets and frogs filled the coolness of the evening with their persistent, throbbing voices. Somewhere a lone whippoorwill sent its mournful cry keening into the night.

It was at times like this that MacKenzie felt a peace he had not known elsewhere in the world, even on the broad oceans or in the high mountains where he'd lived much of his adult life. Like those places, the Florida frontier was a man's country, rich with the promise of growth and renewal, of life and ferment and death. Violent sometimes, even cruel, yet with all of that it was a land filled to the brim with the joy and the wonder of living.

After a time he realized he was not alone.

From the corner of his eye he saw Becky seated nearby, her skirts about her knees and her arms crossed upon them. For long minutes neither spoke, both content to sit quietly watching the ripples on the water amid the deepening shadows of the forest.

When the girl broke the silence at last, her voice was soft in the evening stillness.

"It is beautiful, is it not? Once or twice, walking alone on the heaths of my native Scotland, I have felt something like this. But there the land belonged to others. It could never truly be my own."

John nodded. "No land is our own," he said after a brief pause, "but that we make it our own. When we've left our mark upon the land, when there's somethin' of ourselves in it, only then is it our land."

The young woman turned her face toward him in the fading light. "What is it you mean to leave of yourself in this wilderness, John MacKenzie? For it is clear enough to me that you have chosen this land as your own."

He thought for a moment before replying. "I mean to leave what all men wish to leave behind them, I guess. Somethin' that was not here before, but was within myself." He looked at her.

"I've seen much in my travels, and everywhere man lives it is the same. On the coasts of England and Europe are great towerin' stones o' granite, put up forgotten centuries ago by peoples who left nothin' else o' themselves behind. In Egypt are the pyramids, and in Asia temples of gold by the hundred. In this land are man-made mountains and huge figures o' serpents and birds carved from the livin' earth.

"Some call these monuments to forgotten gods. I believe they are simply monuments to the vision o' man. Whether 'tis a great pyramid in the desert or a small freehold in some green valley, I think each man has the desire to make his own private vision real, and to have those who come after him say, 'There lived a man of vision.'"

He smiled. "Compared to some o' these my own is a modest vision. I mean to build a *rancho* in the Florida wilderness as the Spaniards once did, and to settle down to raisin' beef for the northern colonies. With the aid o' Blackie's treasure, or without it, I'll do that in time. And if Fortune smiles, I'll live out my days on the land watchin' my herds increase and my sons grow tall, perhaps to add their own visions to this land someday."

He fell silent and for a time they sat in the gathering shadows without feeling the need for further words. Then Becky said, "It is a fine vision, John MacKenzie. One that suits you well, I think." She paused briefly. "Yet it seems to me there may be something lacking from all of your well-laid plans. Something to do with the raising of those tall sons . . ."

He glanced at her, but could no longer see her face in the darkness beneath the trees. And yet John had a strange feeling that she was smiling at him.

His eyes opened in the hour before dawn and he lay still as was his custom, listening to the morning sounds. Outside the lean-to a gentle rain was falling, whispering among the leaves of the forest and drumming softly on the canvas above his head.

It was only a mild pre-dawn shower, the kind that typically ended with the sun's rising or shortly afterward. Many times in the past John had awakened with pleasure to the damp coolness of such a morning, pulling his blankets more tightly about his shoulders to await the dawning of a fresh, newly washed day.

On this morning however, he had reason to wish it otherwise. For the sound of the rain masked all others in the forest, making it more difficult to hear if danger should be at hand.

And Tyrone's pursuers were out there somewhere, possibly many miles from this place but perhaps much closer. MacKenzie had a feeling it might be the latter. It was not a feeling he could easily explain, but the steady noise overhead seemed to increase its warning with every minute that passed.

Turning on an elbow to take up his pistol and knife, he looked beyond the shelter into the small clearing beside their camp. Blackie was on guard, huddled in his heavy pea-jacket beneath a large magnolia tree so that the broad waxy leaves would ward off all but the heaviest drops. His pistol lay ready in his lap.

John glanced at the young woman beside him as he sat up to pull on his boots. She was awake, and she smiled when she saw him looking at her. "Good morning," he said, reaching for his buckskin jacket.

"It is, is it not?" She clutched the blankets about her with one hand and sat up, still smiling. "A bit of a damp one I see, but no more so than in the Scottish highlands. Many's the time I've traveled in such weather, and never the worse for it."

"'Twill clear by the dawnin' I think," he replied. "But we will make an early start, no matter the weather. I'll be more easy when we're upon the water and makin' our way downriver." He shrugged on his jacket, then crawled from the shelter and stood up. "Perhaps 'tis only the damp and the dark, but it is an uncomfortable feelin' I have about this place."

As he crossed the clearing to where Blackie sat beneath his sheltering magnolia, John was certain what he felt had nothing to do with the weather. It was something that came of living in the wild. No frontiersman was willing to discount such feelings, for they often meant the difference between life and death.

The seaman shook his head as MacKenzie hunkered down beside him. "'Tis a mornin' for the fishes and those as hunts 'em," the older man said irritably, "nor much fittin' for anythin' else, to my way o' thinkin'." He shivered in the pre-dawn cold and pulled his pea-jacket more tightly about him. "A day like this serves only to make a man appreciate the more a snug harbor, and a drop o' the devil for comfort!"

John smiled. "'Twill be dry and warm enough in a few hours, I believe." He met the other man's eyes. "Though by then I'd imagine you'll be after findin' somethin' else to complain about."

The sailor started to make a sharp reply, but reconsidered. "Lad, you're gettin' to know old Blackie too well I think. Yet since complainin' is one o' the few pleasures in the world that costs nothin', and since it gives me comfort in my old age, I'll thank you to not be deprivin' me of it."

"By all means," John said agreeably, rising to his feet. "Complain to your heart's content. But while you're about it, would you be so good as to give us a hand strikin' the camp and stowin' our goods aboard the raft? By the time the sun is over the trees I want to be some several miles downriver."

Blackie rose and placed the pistol behind his belt. He looked at the other man. "And no tea, is it," he asked quietly, "on a raw wet mornin' like this?"

"No tea for now. I've a desire to be off without delay, and a fire would be devilish hard to start at the moment. We'll pack some earth at one end o' the raft and when the weather clears we'll make a small blaze to heat a pot." John grinned. "For now, just be thankful that you've been given another reason for complainin'."

They packed quickly, and by the time their supplies had been secured aboard the raft the rain had stopped and the day was growing lighter. A thick mist still hung upon the river though, hovering only inches above the dark water and spreading ghostly tendrils over the land so that they could see no more than a dozen yards in any direction.

MacKenzie took a position behind the raft, with Blackie and Becky on either side. With some effort they managed to push and drag the heavy craft across the damp grass to the river's edge. Here they paused a minute to rest, then took hold again to move their burden over the sandy bank and into the water.

Suddenly John stopped and lifted a hand to halt the others. He rose and backed slowly away from the shore, motioning his companions to do the same. Then, drawing and gently cocking his pistol, he pointed toward a moving object a short distance upstream.

Blackie and Becky looked where the frontiersman pointed, and could make out a sinuous brown shape undulating slowly through the calmer water near the shore. A small wake spread behind the serpent's ugly wedge-shaped head as it glided wraithlike through the dark current.

When it had passed them by on its way down the river Becky opened her mouth to speak, but John quickly raised a finger to his lips for silence. An instant later a second serpent appeared, cleaving the water in gentle wavelets a few yards behind the first.

As the second snake disappeared downstream Mackenzie took a deep breath and his muscles relaxed slowly, but he did not replace the pistol in his belt.

"Water moccasins," he said in a low voice. "Venomous and deadly as the rattlesnake, but far more dangerous to my mind. For they're ill-tempered creatures who'll attack upon the slightest provocation, and give no warnin' at all o' their intentions. They're not shy like other serpents, but have been known to chase after a man, on land well as in the water." He looked at his companions.

"You must be on the watch for such as these whenever you're near water in this country. Leave them be as you would any other creature in the wild, if you can. But do not hesitate to kill if you are attacked, for their bite is swift and deadly."

Blackie took his eyes slowly from the mist-shrouded river and squinted at the frontiersman. "Aye," he said, "if I see one o' those before it sees me, you've no need to concern yourself on my account, lad. I'd not waste about tryin' to uncover its intentions, if y' catch my drift. An ounce o' prevention, as they say . . ."

The seaman fell suddenly silent. John glanced at him and felt a prickling sensation at the back of his neck. For he saw that Blackie was looking past him toward a fog-shrouded stand of cypress a short distance downstream. The expression on his face was not pleasant.

Turning slowly, MacKenzie saw three men standing

at the edge of the clearing. The mist clinging about their legs made them appear like ghostly apparitions in the early morning light. They were several feet apart, as well separated as the small area beside the river permitted. And all of them held weapons.

John recognized his own Pennsylvania rifle in the hands of the tall man at the center. Its muzzle was slightly down but he could see the hammer pulled back ready to fire. The two men on either side held cocked pistols, leveled steadily at John and Blackie.

The man in the center John knew as the one he had knocked to the ground in the courtyard of the inn at St. Augustine. His burly companion of that evening was on his right.

MacKenzie's eyes flicked briefly to the third man, a short lean fellow with a thin face and constantly shifting eyes. This might well be the most dangerous of the three, he thought. For there was something in this man's eyes which said he was not only ready to kill, but wanted to kill. In addition to the pistol in his hand there was a long knife at his belt, the length of a man's forearm.

14

JOHN STILL HELD HIS OWN PISTOL in his hand, cocked and ready from their encounter with the moccasins a few minutes earlier. As he took a cautious step backward away from the raft, he held it low against his leg, hoping it might not be easily seen in the surrounding fog.

He spoke quietly, the slightest hint of a smile playing at the corners of his lips. "A good mornin' to you, gentlemen. It seems you've traveled far since last we met." He was already thinking about what the black slave-hunter Jeremiah had told them a few days earlier. There had been *five* in the pursuing party. Where were the others?

MacKenzie glanced toward the high bank on his right. There was a faint whisper of leaves as a bird suddenly flew up to an overhanging branch. One of them, at least. The Indian? Or LeBeau? They might be together, but one might as easily be elsewhere. Perhaps hidden in the woods at their back.

"Far enough," the tall man answered, "in this God-forsaken wilderness. But well worth the trouble and the journey I think now, for you've none of you been far from my thoughts. I'd a great longing to see each of you, one more time." He nodded to the sailor. "It has been some little while has it not, Blackie?"

"Aye, Jack, it has that." The seaman's face was grim, yet his gaze was steady as he met the tall man's eyes. "Other times, other customs, Jack. I'd be a liar if I said I've missed your company." John saw that the older man had hooked his thumbs in his belt while he spoke, moving them imperceptibly toward the pistol hidden at the small of his back.

"Ah, Blackie, Blackie," the other said, shaking his head, "'tis a shame you've so little regard for an old shipmate. I'm pained to the quick. Myself, I have looked forward to this meeting for some time now." His face twisted into a hard smile. "'Twill be a pleasure to see you lying on the ground with a ball in your guts, pouring your blood out upon the grass." He turned to MacKenzie.

"And you as well, my lad. It's something I owe you for your work of a week ago." The tall man raised his left hand to his jaw and rubbed it tenderly. "Two teeth lost, and a painful hour in the barber's chair . . ."

Suddenly MacKenzie moved. He threw himself to his left, firing into Bill Simms' thick body as he did, then hit the ground rolling to come up catlike in a low crouch with his knife in his hand. A pistol ball whipped by his ear as he came off the ground, followed by the sound of a shot, and then an instant later, two more.

Thatcher's left arm was spouting blood. Simms was down. John looked quickly toward where the third man had stood, but for the moment could not see him in the thick fog and the smoke that now blanketed the small clearing.

His move had been calculated to take the bad men by surprise, and to spoil their shooting. It had accomplished both. They were distracted by Thatcher's talk, and the extra few seconds of reaction time — plus the fact that it was harder for a right-handed man to shift his aim to the right than to the left — had made the difference.

MacKenzie had also counted on Blackie being ready, and the sailor had not disappointed. Almost at the same moment that Ben Pike fired at MacKenzie and missed, the seaman's heavy ball had struck the hard leather shot case at Thatcher's side and glanced upward

LEE GRAMLING

to shatter the tall man's forearm when he lowered it to grip the rifle.

Bill Simms was sitting on the grass, knocked backward by the force of a half-inch ball fired at point-blank range. His pistol had gone off into the ground as he fell. He was looking down at the red stain spreading over his shiny satin shirt-front now with an odd expression on his face.

Acrid smoke filled the clearing, mingling with the fog to make visibility almost impossible. Suddenly, John saw the hatchet-faced man emerge from the mists, advancing carefully with the long dagger in his hand. He circled around MacKenzie toward the river and John had no choice but to turn with him. Yet as he did he called over his shoulder to his companions:

"The Indian! Above you and to the right! —And LeBeau! God knows where . . ."

Blackie turned, unarmed, to face the bluff MacKenzie had indicated. An instant later there was a flash of movement and the native leapt from the trees, his knife gleaming in his hand. A rifle boomed from the forest behind him and the red man twisted suddenly in midair, crying out and collapsing in a heap at the sailor's feet. His hips rose once in a shuddering convulsion, and he lay still.

John had only a glimpse of all this, and no time to wonder where the unexpected rifle-shot had come from. For at that instant the man with the dagger sprang at him.

His enemy was several inches shorter than MacKen-

176

zie, and some twenty pounds lighter. But the length of his blade more than made up for the difference in reach, and he was clearly no stranger to knife-fighting. Quick as a cat, the man advanced easily with his weapon low, its needle-sharp point raised to strike upward at the soft parts of the body.

John twisted to evade the first assault, and was almost too slow. When he moved to grasp the other man's knife-arm his opponent slipped eellike from his grip and backed quickly away. For a long minute they circled warily, each watching for an opening.

MacKenzie feinted, but barely managed to pull his hand back in time to avoid serious injury. As it was the sleeve of his jacket was laid open and a thin red line showed on the white fabric beneath. He'd been considered a fast man in some circles, but in that moment John knew he was no match for this man's lightninglike speed.

Pike's move had forced MacKenzie back so quickly that he stumbled and almost fell. Whirling to avoid a fatal thrust, he managed to slap the other's blade aside and turn full around, backing up rapidly to give himself more room.

His opponent advanced unhurriedly, still cautious and watchful, though a twisted grin now drew his lips into a thin bloodless arc. The smaller man moved sideways, feinting once, and then again. John kept his eyes constantly on those of his enemy, seeking out the man's intentions an instant before his knife-arm could respond.

He would need every bit of that reaction time, for

he knew now that the slightest hesitation would mean his death. He had to find an advantage quickly, before he began to tire and his own movements slowed even more.

He had been retreating toward the edge of the clearing, forced back slowly by the other man's deft thrusts and slashes. Suddenly in the thick mist at the forest's edge John felt a branch scratch his back. He decided instantly that his chance, if he were to have one, was now. Feinting only a trifle obviously, he straightened quickly and drew back.

Ben Pike hesitated a fraction of a second, wary of the expected return thrust and perhaps a bit unsure in the poor visibility caused by the dense fog and smoke. In that moment MacKenzie ducked beneath the branch that had been pressed backward by his last movement. The limb lashed at the smaller man's face and John followed it in, grasping Pike's wrist and shoving it out of line with his body while he drove his own knife violently upward.

The two grappled desperately for several seconds, and then MacKenzie twisted the large knife in his enemy's belly and saw the other man's eyes begin to glaze. At last the dagger fell from Pike's limp fingers and he slumped to the ground.

John quickly withdrew his knife from the lifeless body at his feet and turned to face the clearing. As he knelt to peer through the smoke and the mist however, it seemed the battle was already over.

Three bodies lay on the damp grass, unmoving. The Indian and Bill Simms appeared dead, as well as Pike. Blackie was taking his pistol back from Becky, who had remained in the middle of the clearing throughout the fight, calmly reloading. As MacKenzie thrust his knife into the ground to clean it, he saw the tall buckskin-clad figure of Jeremiah step from the forest, his rifle in his hands.

"Had a feelin' you might could use a bit of help," the black man said as John rose to approach him. "So I just come on along to see what I could see."

"Our thanks to you," John said, taking the other's hand. "You're a welcome sight, and no mistake. But I'll confess I might not have expected it after our last conversation. For then it seemed you fought only for profit, and there's little enough o' that in aidin' fugitives."

Jeremiah shook his head. "Don't make much sense at that, does it? Reckon I didn't think much o' the odds, and I just wanted to see how matters would turn out if they was a bit more even-up. Then again, maybe . . ." He glanced quickly in Becky's direction. "Well, maybe I just figured you-all might be too good-a folks to die at the hands of the likes o' these."

"Whatever your reasons," John said, clapping the other man on the shoulder, "you have our gratitude."

"*De nada*," Jeremiah answered with a shrug, "as the Spaniard says. You know that boy I was chasin' got clean away from me anyhow, couple o' days ago. I'd nothin' much else needed doin' right away." He grinned "And I reckon a man's got a right to a well-meanin' act onct in a while, 'long as he don't go around makin' a habit of it."

The sun was up by now, and the fog was beginning to clear. With a sudden thought MacKenzie looked around them.

"Whatever became of that tall man who seemed to be the leader of our pursuers?" he asked. "And LeBeau? I saw naught at all of him durin' the fight."

"I trailed five from the tradin' post," Jeremiah said. "But those three was the only ones I ever saw after I got here." He indicated the bodies. "Never had a glimpse of the other two since last night."

"Aye." Blackie nodded. "Them, and Jack Thatcher, was all I saw myself. No one else from the beginnin' to now. Jack was hit bad. I imagine he up and weighed anchor soon as he got a taste o' how the wind was blowin'."

MacKenzie nodded, frowning. It was likely enough the injured Thatcher had lost his stomach for battle and had gone off to lick his wounds. LeBeau's disappearance might be understood too, if he saw no personal profit in the fight. He was known to be a man of few loyalties, though brave enough when attacked, or when there was something he wanted badly enough for himself.

Still, it was not a comforting thought that two such dangerous men were now abroad in the wilderness, their whereabouts unknown. Each alone would be an adversary to be reckoned with if he chose to continue the chase. And with a hundred guineas at stake, there might be others.

"We'd best leave here straightway," John said after a moment. "Whether or not we've seen the last of those two, I'd not care to meet any more chance visitors before breakfast."

"Aye, lad." Blackie replaced his pistol in his belt and began gathering up the dead men's weapons. "I'm with you. It was a near enough thing at that, this mornin's work. Had you not moved and shot when you did we might all have slipped our cables by now." He straightened from his task and glanced at the frontiersman.

"Gave me a turn, though, it did. When you moved so sudden-like in the face o' drawn pistols an' all, not even sayin' aye, nay or by your leave!"

"Thatcher and his friends meant to kill us," John said, "and were surely makin' no secret about it. Yet the tall man seemed to feel the need for a lengthy discourse upon the matter." He shrugged. "Myself, I couldna see the sense o' talkin' when it was fightin' that needed to be done."

He sheathed his knife and recovered his pistol from Becky, then took a second pistol from the sailor, shoving both into his belt, one on either side. Then he turned to Jeremiah.

"I expect the horses and outfits of these men will be somewhere about. We've enough for our needs, and we've no time to be huntin' through the forest in any case. So you're welcome to the lot, whatever LeBeau and Thatcher may not have taken with them. Our thanks again for your help." John grasped the slave-hunter's hand firmly, and turned to join Blackie and Becky at the raft.

"Might's well give you a hand with that while I'm about it," the black man said, hesitating only briefly. "I'm not in so big a hurry to be away." He joined the three of them, taking a position behind the heavy logs while MacKenzie took hold of one side and Blackie and Becky the other. In a few minutes they had managed to manhandle the unwieldy craft over the bank and into the water.

"She floats, at least," the sailor said, rinsing his hands in the water at his waist and stepping back to survey their handiwork. "Though I'll admit I've shipped aboard trimmer vessels in my day." He grinned at the girl beside him. "All the same, 'twill take us to where we're goin' and that's what matters now."

John climbed aboard, then looked at the Negro on the shore. "Again, our thanks," he said. "Have a care, and keep well."

"Aye, I'll do that. And you as well." Jeremiah turned, a bit reluctantly it seemed, and started away from the river. The sound of Blackie's shout brought him back around in an instant.

"Lass, look out!" There was a sudden violent thrashing beside the raft where the sailor and Becky had stood, the dark water churning as the seaman backed away wrestling with a thick serpentine body that had fixed itself to his upper arm.

MacKenzie leapt toward his companion, knife in

hand. But he slipped and lost his footing on the bobbing logs. As he fell to his knees he saw that the slave-hunter was already in the water at Blackie's side.

Jeremiah's blade flashed once and the moccasin was decapitated. Lifting the writhing body high over his head, the black man flung it far off into the swift-moving current. Then, picking the sailor up as though he weighed no more than a sack of grain, he carried him from the river and laid him gently on the grassy bank.

"A tourniquet!" John called to Becky as she followed them ashore. "Tear a strip o' cloth and tie it tight beneath his armpit to stop the poison's spread!" He was securing the raft and moving to join them as he spoke.

Jeremiah wasted no time, kneeling at once to cut away the sailor's jacket and shirt-sleeve at the shoulder. He located the ugly red welts where the fangs had entered the muscle of the arm, and made two deft incisions in each with the razor-sharp point of his knife. Blackie grunted faintly as the blade bit deep. His skin was already turning pale and clammy from the shock of the wound.

When the blood began to flow MacKenzie reached under the seaman's armpit and pressed his thumb up hard against the vein. Keeping his hand there, he helped Becky fix the tourniquet firmly, then moved the knot around to take the place of his thumb. The Negro was already sucking the venom from the incisions with his mouth and spitting it out on the grass at his feet.

With luck, enough of the poison would be gotten

out in this way so that the sailor's chances of survival might be improved. It was all that could be done, and John himself could do no more.

He rose and took a step back, watching Becky. The girl's face was pale and her eyes were wide as she knelt beside the still figure on the ground. But there were no tears, and the hands that had tied the tourniquet had been as steady as his own.

This, he thought, is truly a woman to ride the river with. A steady woman, one who'd stay by a man no matter what came. At that moment he felt a fierce pride, yet one he realized he had no right to. For there had been no words between them. No words at all, about . . .

Becky's eyes lifted to meet his and John felt a sudden embarrassment, as though she could read his thoughts. But all she said was, "There is a bit of brandy among the things on the raft. I can fetch it if you think it will do him good."

"To drink, no," he answered. "Not yet at any rate. Brandy warms the blood, and so might serve only to make the poison spread faster. Yet do you fetch it, for 'twill be good to wash the wound with before we bandage it."

Jeremiah spat and turned his head toward her. "Aye," he said, "and a small dram for m'self, too, if you don't mind. 'Tis a bitter taste I've got in my mouth from this, and a drop o' good spirits to wash it out with would be a blessin'."

While the girl walked to the raft, taking more care

than usual to watch where she stepped, MacKenzie looked questioningly at the slave-hunter. Jeremiah shrugged and sat back on his heels.

"I believe I have much of it out," he said, "but the strike is high up the arm, near the body. A tough man might survive, and this is a tough man. But only time will tell."

John nodded, then knelt beside the other man. "When we've bandaged him and you've had your drop o' brandy," he said, "I'll ask you to help me get him aboard the raft. He'll fare no worse upon the water I believe, and there is still good reason for us to be some miles from here before nightfall."

"I'll help you with that," Jeremiah said, "and gladly. But what then? Y' must sleep sometime, and yet now you've no one else to keep watch through the night."

He seemed to study the ground in front of him for a long time before continuing. "Might be," he said at last, "y' could use another pair of eyes to see you through this last part o' your journey."

MacKenzie regarded the slave-hunter thoughtfully. "Are y' offerin'?" he asked after a moment.

"I am." Jeremiah nodded. "If you'll have me."

John considered, then responded, "I can promise you no profit from this venture, y' understand. Nothin' at all for your trouble but our thanks, and perhaps a lonely grave in the wilderness when you've done with it all."

The black man met the frontiersman's eyes. "I know

that," he said, "and I've asked for nothin' else." He paused, then added, "I'm a proud man, John MacKenzie, a man of honor, no matter what you may think o' my choice for makin' a livin'. My offer was freely made. Accept it freely as it was intended, or else let it be."

John lowered his head. Gradually a slow smile spread across his face. "Done," he said after a moment. "Done." He rose and clapped the other man on the back. "And with my thanks, Jeremiah. It's proud we'll be to have you with us!"

Becky brought the brandy and a piece of clean linen to dress the sailor's wound, and when they had done this they all shared a cup between them. The girl grimaced as the liquor burned her throat, but she smiled as she replaced the stopper in the dark-green bottle.

"I'll save the rest for Blackie now," she said. "Belike he'll be wantin' a drop when he wakes."

"Aye," John agreed, "'twill do him good."

Then he added to himself, more softly, "If he wakes."

15 ⚡

To say that JACK THATCHER was angry would be to completely understate the seething depths of his rage at this instant.

What should have been a ridiculously simple matter, once they had finally run MacKenzie and his party to ground, had somehow turned to disaster in the blinking of an eye. All that was needed was to fire two shots, finish the business with knives if need be, and grab the woman. By now they would be well on their way back to St. Augustine, leaving this godforsaken wilderness behind for what meager comforts that provincial capital afforded.

What, by the eternal fires of hell, had happened? Damn it, they'd had both men under their guns!

The bone in his left arm was shattered, smashed to bits by the impact of Blackie's pistol shot. Thatcher had suspected it at once, and a glance was all he needed to confirm his suspicion when he'd stopped to splint and bandage the wound soon after the battle. That was several hours ago. Now the shock had worn off and his arm hurt wretchedly with every step the black stallion took. He realized, but refused to consider, the probability that he would never again have full use of that arm.

Thatcher's pain and the unexpected defeat by the men they had pursued would have been more than enough to fuel his ready ire and thirst for revenge. But there was something more. For when the shooting had started, and ever since that time, he had seen nothing at all of Jacob LeBeau.

A hard life on the nether edge of society had long ago blunted whatever conscience Jack Thatcher might once have had. There was little in the way of evil and corruption he had not seen and experienced in this world, and there were few vices he had not himself participated in, more than once.

Cruelty he understood and accepted as a way of life. Drunkenness, brawling, wenching — with or without the wench's consent — treachery, revenge, murder . . . All of these and more were in Thatcher's repertoire, and they were common enough among those with whom he associated. In his way Jack Thatcher was a tolerant man, for long ago he had learned to overlook most moral failings in himself and others.

Cowardice, however, was not included among these.

And no matter what else might be said, there was little doubt in Thatcher's mind that LeBeau had acted the part of the coward. He'd abandoned his comrades in battle, and this was perhaps the only mortal sin a man like Thatcher still recognized, and would not forgive.

He nodded in the saddle and his eyes closed briefly, but then he jerked himself erect, clutching at the horse's mane to keep himself from falling. He had lost blood, and there was a weakness upon him. But as he forced his thoughts back to the half-breed who had abandoned them in the clearing his rage returned tenfold, giving him all the fierce will he needed to overcome his body's demands.

"You will pay him," Tyrone had said, "in cold steel." And with an unnatural strength born of his fury and his passion for revenge, Jack Thatcher meant to make that payment. He meant to make it soon, and in full — if he never took another breath beyond that moment.

The sun was well past the midway point. He had been riding for hours, though he was scarcely aware of the passage of time. His world now was made up entirely of trees and Spanish moss, of sweltering heat and buzzing insects, and of the chipped earth on the forest floor where LeBeau's horse had passed not long before.

Thatcher was no tracker, but he was an intelligent man and had paid careful attention each time the half-breed had paused to read the signs of their quarry. At present, LeBeau's trail offered no special difficulties. He had obviously not expected to be followed, and had made no particular effort to conceal his passing. No one had used this trail for some weeks evidently, for the only marks on the ground were those left behind by the big frontiersman's mount.

They had crossed the river not far from the scene of the battle, and Thatcher could tell from periodic glimpses of the sun through the trees that the other was now riding steadily toward the south and west. There seemed to be a deliberate purpose to his movement, for he had paused only briefly to rest his horse, or to let it drink from time to time.

LeBeau had no doubt concluded, as Jack Thatcher had from the raft they'd seen, that MacKenzie meant to travel by water to his final destination. Evidently the half-breed intended to intercept them at some point further downstream. His final purpose could only be guessed at, but no doubt it involved some personal plans for the treasure, or the girl, or both.

That sort of treachery was something Thatcher might have done himself, and he found the idea itself neither surprising nor particularly hateful in the nature of it. But he had no intention of allowing it to happen, for there was a more pressing issue to be dealt with here. There was a debt of blood to be paid for the half-breed's earlier treachery. A debt the tall man meant to exact before the dawning of even one more day.

Afterward . . . ? Afterward, if he survived, Jack Thatcher might at last take stock and begin to make some plans of his own for the future.

Day faded slowly into twilight on the broad river of the San Juanito. The shadows of the moss-laden trees grew longer and a few stars appeared, winking to life beside the silver disc of the moon. Frogs and crickets were already filling the air with their evening serenade.

MacKenzie stood at the back of the raft, guiding their course by gently sculling with the long pole. He was tired to the bone after the battle and the long hours on the water, but there would be little rest now until they reached their destination.

There was still the chance of pursuit, from LeBeau, Thatcher, perhaps others. And there were the dangers of the wilderness itself. As they neared the coast especially, they must be on the watch for alligators. In this area they were known to hunt in packs, and the saltwater variety was even larger and more ravenous than its cousin of the lakes and streams.

Blackie slept fitfully beneath the palmetto thatch a few feet away, muttering from time to time in his delirium. Becky had remained with him constantly, though there was little she or anyone else could do now to help.

The poison was in the sailor's body, and he was fighting it as best he could. His fate was in the hands of Providence.

Jeremiah sat quietly at the front of the raft with his arms across his knees, studying the river and the growing shadows around them. He had remained like that for hours, unmoving as an ebony statue. MacKenzie knew the slave-hunter's senses were as wise to the ways of this Florida land as his own, and he was more relieved than he cared to admit that the Negro had chosen to join them for this last leg of their journey. He'd a feeling their troubles were not over yet, and all of them might be grateful for their new comrade's help before this trip was done.

He did not like keeping their final goal secret from their new companion, but did not feel free to reveal it without consulting the others. And there had been no opportunity for that. The matter might prove academic in any case, since only Blackie knew the location of the treasure and there was no guarantee that the old sailor would ever be able to guide them to it.

Privately, MacKenzie still harbored some doubts about the matter anyway. He'd heard many tales of buried treasure, but none he'd ever discovered to be true. Men who came by gold honestly were more likely to save it or invest it. Those who gained it by other means could rarely resist the temptation to spend it.

But the gold coin the seaman had produced was real enough, and perhaps the venture would turn out as hoped. Since Becky had been willing — even enthusiastic — at the prospect, John had agreed readily, admitting to himself that he had little to lose in his present circumstances. And once he had undertaken a task, it was never his habit to shy from seeing it to a conclusion.

Jeremiah stirred, and looked around at MacKenzie. A moment later the slave-hunter rose and made his way aft.

"Might's well spell you a bit," he said when they were close enough so that he could speak in low tones. "Don't much feel like sleepin' myself, and I reckon I ought to make myself useful. Imagine you could do with a bit of a rest."

"Aye." MacKenzie nodded. "For a few hours, perhaps." He handed the pole to the other and started forward, skirting the palmetto shelter and making his way to the front of the raft. As he was about to stretch out on the blankets there, he turned and saw Becky watching him from the opening in the shelter. He moved back beside her.

"He's sleeping now," she said when John drew near. "It's little enough rest he's gotten this day, with the tossing and the turning in his fever. And he's talked much too, though little that made any kind of sense to me."

MacKenzie knew Blackie's past might provide some clues to their present dangers, especially the connection with Thatcher and Tyrone — evident enough, though unexplained, from recent events. "What sort of things did he talk about?" he asked quietly.

"Several times he mentioned a girl, one who appears to have suffered some awful fate, for he grows almost frantic whenever he speaks of her." Becky paused. "Other times he spoke of a flag, and used a word I did not understand. It sounded like 'filbert' or something like that." She looked at John. "A name, perhaps?"

"Perhaps." MacKenzie shrugged. As a name it meant nothing to him, but who knew what a man might think of, real or unreal, once the fever was upon him? "What else did he say?"

"Little I could find meaning in. Some battles at sea I think. And perhaps some wilder times ashore." She smiled slightly.

"No other names? No mention of people or past connections?"

"No. None that I could make out." Becky paused. "He spoke of the flag often. It seemed to be something of importance to him. Sailing under the flag. Sailing under the dark flag. Or under the . . ."

John looked at her. "The black flag?" he asked softly.

She nodded, puzzled. "Yes, that's it. The black flag. He mentioned it time and time again."

The black flag. . . Filbert . . . Of course. John nodded. "'Tis clear enough then," he said after a moment. "In his sickness our friend has perhaps said more than he wished anyone to know. It seems he has been speakin' o' the brotherhood o' the black flag. Pirates. Freebooters. Filibusters, the Spanish call them." He paused in thought. "I wonder now if . . ."

"Aye, lad." The voice from the palmetto shelter was weak, but easily heard in the night air. "You've figured it right enough. Now you know old Blackie's darkest secret."

At the sound Becky and John both turned, then moved closer to the pallet where the sick man lay.

"Seems almost a dream now," the sailor went on, "though 'twas real enough I fear. Near half my thirty years on the green water, robbin', killin', plunderin'." Blackie was struggling to sit up. When Becky tried to make him lie back he shook his head weakly and grasped John's arm.

"No, lass, let me be for a bit. It's somethin's been eatin' at my craw for a long while. I'd as soon speak of it now amongst friends, while I've still the breath to do it." With MacKenzie supporting him, he rose to a sitting position and looked at each of his companions in turn. Then he went on in a quiet but steady voice:

"I take no pride in sayin' it now, but for a time the life had its appeal. We fought, and we killed, but I told m'self the others had their chance, same as us. More guns and men than us, often as not. It seemed fair to me, who never had nothin' since the day I was weaned, to take what I wanted from those who hadn't the guts or the skill to hold it for themselves. 'Twas a bold life, I told m'self, an' a free one. A man's life the way I looked at it." He paused. "Until . . ." Blackie closed his eyes.

"First I ever saw of her she was backed up on the fantail of a Portugee merchantman. Little slip of a thing, hardly more'n a child. Pretty. Big eyes, dark hair. Full o' fire and spit she was, darin' the lot of us. Couple o' men laughed, but nobody made a move to take her. Like turned to stone they was, an' me with 'em . . ."

He took a slow breath. "After a bit she looked all around an' kind o' shook her head like she was disgusted wi' the lot of us. Then she turned, and jumped off right into the blue water."

Blackie was silent for a long time, and the sound of crickets was loud in the night. "Sharks," he said at last. "Sharks . . . didn't leave nothin' at all, but that long black hair, floatin' out on the bloody water . . ."

John and Becky said nothing, for there was nothing to be said. After a while the sailor opened his eyes and shook his head. "That's when I left the freebooter's life, left it for good. Might 'a left the sea too right then, on'y I'd no other way to support m'self. Never done much o' anythin' else."

He looked at the girl in the moonlight. "She favored you a bit, now 't I think on it. Maybe . . ."

Becky nodded. "Maybe it wasn't completely an accident, when you stepped between the serpent and myself?" She squeezed his arm gently. "I suspected as much. And I suspect that you've never really been the bad man you thought you were, Blackie Teague."

"Thanks, lass." The sailor spoke softly. "Thanks for sayin' that at least, whether it be true or not."

John was only half paying attention now. He was deep in thought. "So it is pirate treasure we're after?" he asked after a moment. "The wages o' murder and robbery on the high seas?"

"Aye," Blackie answered. "It is. An' them it was took from'll never miss it, I'm sorry to say. We've all as much right to it as anybody else, save those who put it there· Dread Jamie Tyrone and his murderin' crew!"

John looked at the old seaman in naked surprise "Tyrone," he said, then nodded. "Aye, so that's where I knew the name. It's been some years since I heard it, but there was a time he flew the black flag off the China coast, was there not?"

"Aye, and in the Indian Ocean and the Arab Seas as well. He always took great care to do his raidin' on the other side o' the world."

"Yet now he is in the Floridas." MacKenzie frowned. "For what purpose, I wonder?"

"I would 'a thought that would be obvious, lad. Blackie's voice was weakening, but his eyes burned brightly at the question. "He's made his fortune, an' now he wants the rest of it: power, respectability, position. Like Morgan before him, Tyrone seeks forgiveness from the Crown for his sins — and a governorship. He means to be the next governor of East Florida!"

"And the treasure?"

"Only a part of his take, but a large part. When Tyrone first heard the news this was to be a British colony he laid a course for the Caribbean and buried two large chests here against future need. 'Twas an investment, like, in Dread Jamie's future ambitions."

John had more questions, but when he looked the sailor's eyes were closed and he was breathing regularly. Becky tucked the blankets about the sleeping man's chest and MacKenzie made his way to the front of the raft, and his own uneasy rest.

16 🌿

JACK THATCHER DREW BACK WEAKLY on the reins in the growing twilight and slumped forward in the saddle until his right hand rested on the big black's damp neck. The horse had needed little encouragement to call a halt. It was a fine animal, but plantation-bred and unused to constant travel in the wilderness. The coarse grasses of the Florida scrub country were very different from its usual diet, and there had been few opportunities to sample even that rough forage. The tall man had been riding hard since early morning, and his horse was almost used up.

Thatcher himself was nearer to being spent than he cared to admit. He was a tough man, but the hot ride and the loss of blood had taken their toll. After a moment he closed his eyes and his head dropped forward against his chest. For several long minutes he sat like that in the gathering gloom of the hardwood hammock where he and his mount had paused to rest.

Then, with a deliberate effort, he straightened in the saddle and shook his head to clear it. Looking around him, the tall man scowled angrily. He had hoped to catch up with LeBeau long before this.

They had been following a narrow sand trail through dense swamps for several hours, crossing innumerable small creeks and skirting treacherous marshes on every side. The chances of continuing after dark in such country without becoming lost or drowning in some hidden bog were too great to be ignored. Yet Thatcher was unwilling to abandon his pursuit. By morning he would be weaker, and perhaps feverish from his wound as well.

Throwing a leg over the animal's back, he slid wearily to the ground. The moon was up, and the white sand path could be seen faintly among the deeper shadows of the forest floor. He would try walking and leading his horse for a while. Perhaps he could manage to keep to the trail on foot, and the black would gain something from not having to carry him.

Grimly Thatcher placed one foot before the other, forcing himself not to think beyond the next trudging step.

He had no idea how far he had walked in the sucking sand and the moonlight before he became aware of a dim orange glow among the trees. Unbelieving at first, he stopped to rub his eyes with the fingers of his right hand. When he looked again the glow was still there, a short distance ahead and to his left.

It seemed to be a campfire, flickering faintly among the scrub and palmetto brakes of a small hammock some fifty yards off the trail. Indians, possibly. But Thatcher had an idea that it was not. And he very much wanted it to be the camp of someone else.

He tethered the black to some nearby bushes and knelt for a time to study the light. There was no movement near it that he could see, but that meant little since the area was well-hidden among trees and thick undergrowth. Still, it was late and LeBeau had expected no one to follow him. With luck the frontiersman might be sleeping.

Jack Thatcher checked his weapons carefully. His pistol he recharged and cocked before shoving it into his sash on the left side. He carried a large hunting knife in a scabbard at his back, and now he unsheathed this blade and positioned it in the sling which held his left arm, where it could be grasped easily with his free hand.

Finally he took MacKenzie's rifle from the back of his horse, and with a certain amount of difficulty, owing to his wound, wiped it carefully clean before priming and cocking it. The long firearm would be awkward to handle with only one hand, but in Thatcher's mind two shots were always better than one. A matter of simple insurance.

His fatigue was gone now. His senses had become keenly alert during his preparations, sharpened by the anticipation of exacting a bloody and well-deserved revenge on the man who had shown the white feather that morning when his comrades needed him.

Again he studied the woods between himself and the campfire's glow. His eyes had long since adjusted to the darkness, and, as even a small fire seems unusually bright under such conditions, Thatcher could see far more than one used to town living might think. He took his time, wanting no slip-ups between his intention and the deed at this point in the game.

With infinite care he planned his approach to the nearby hammock, considering all possibilities. There seemed to be one dry passage, but it was likely to be covered with fallen leaves like most of the forest floor hereabouts. A silent approach would be impossible on such a surface, and a single careless noise could well prove fatal with a man like LeBeau in earshot.

Finally he decided on a route that would take him through a small winding creek to within a few yards of the fire. Silent movement in the water would be difficult, but it could be done if a man was careful and did not become impatient. As Thatcher was a cautious and determined man, with some experience in stealthy approaches by water, patience was not a problem in this case.

Resting the barrel of the long rifle on his right shoulder with his hand on the action ready to pull it down beneath his arm and fire instantly, the tall man rose and made his way to the sandy bank of the creek. Easing into the water with slow and deliberate movements, he started downstream, waiting perhaps as much as thirty seconds before moving each foot past the next.

It might take an hour or more to reach the half-breed's camp in this manner, but time was of no importance to Thatcher now. When the matter was settled, and only then, would there be time to think of other things.

At last he had advanced to within a few yards of the camp, yet still hidden from it behind the broad fans of a nearby stand of palmettos. Thatcher halted and stood unmoving for several minutes, calf-deep in the cold water and breathing easily. Now was no time to let his eagerness for the kill get the better of him. An icy calm settled over him. Only a few minutes longer . . .

The fire had burned down to glowing coals, and its light was very faint. That was a good sign, Thatcher thought, for a waking man would surely have continued to add fuel throughout the night. He looked all around him and took a firmer grip on the action of the rifle. Then, hearing and seeing nothing to suggest that his foe might still be on guard, he dropped the stock under his arm and stepped silently from the water, mounting the slight rise of the hammock in two long strides.

Moving quickly around the palmetto bush, the muzzle of the rifle lowered so as to fire instantly into a sleeping form on the ground, Jack Thatcher entered the small clearing on cat feet. For a long moment he stood looking down at the bedroll before him.

It was empty.

Without a doubt it was LeBeau's. Thatcher recognized it immediately, and the battered coffee pot beside the coals as well. But of the big half-breed he saw nothing at all.

With a growing sense of panic, the tall man lifted his eyes and looked about him, unsure what to do. He still held the rifle, and now turned awkwardly to sweep the surrounding woods with it. The shadows of the hammock were dark and still.

He ought to drop the long gun and draw his pistol, he thought suddenly. He could not hope to bring the rifle to bear quickly on a target that might appear from any direction. But then another thought came to him, pushing the first aside with compelling urgency.

He ought to get out of here. Now. This was not the way he had planned things at all. To approach a sleeping man and shoot into him in his bedroll was one thing. To stand there in the glow of the coals with a man of LeBeau's deadly skill waiting for him out there in the dark was something else entirely.

Turning, still undecided whether to keep the rifle or

drop it, Thatcher took two quick steps back the way he had come. The sound of the half-breed's voice froze him to the spot.

"A bit late to come calling. Don't you think?" The voice came from the direction of a large magnolia some dozen yards away. Thatcher thought he saw the man's hulking form next to it, but could not be sure. He hesitated.

"I've been listening to your approach for almost an hour now," LeBeau went on. "Took your time, I'll say that for you. Careful. But not half so careful, or so quiet, as you thought you were. Could learn a thing or two from the Indians in these parts, you know. If you had the time . . ."

Time. There was no more time. The darker shadow beside the tree must be LeBeau. Thatcher raised the rifle, leaning far back to bring its muzzle up in line with his target.

There was a brief hiss, followed by two short flashes in the dark and then a deafening boom! The tall man saw it all, the spark, the ignition of the primer and the muzzle of a pistol spitting fire, slowly, as though time had stood still for that one deadly instant. Then there was a pressure in his chest, and the sound of Thatcher's own weapon discharging as he fell backward to the ground.

He was staring up at the moonlit leaves over his head. He could not recall how he had come to be there on the soft earth. He coughed, and there was a salty taste in his mouth. Blood. *His* blood. Then the tracker was standing over him.

"Had it in mind all along. Saw it in your eyes that first night at my place, but you was never the man for it. Saw that too, right from the start."

Thatcher tried to speak, to answer, to curse his killer, but he suddenly found himself choking on his own blood. His eyes blazed with hatred for the big half-breed. But LeBeau did not see. He was already starting to gather up his things.

"Might's well be on my way now," the frontiersman said, as though to himself. "Can't get a decent night's sleep with all this going on anyhow. Might's well get on down the river."

Those were the last words that Jack Thatcher ever heard.

Night enclosed the travelers in solitude on the dark waters of the river. Only the occasional cry of a hunting owl could be heard, and once the angry screech of a bobcat shouting its defiance into the night.

MacKenzie came awake and after a moment he rose to a sitting position at the bow of the raft. With his arms around his knees he sat listening to the sounds of the forest for several long minutes. A glance aft had shown that Jeremiah was still at the helm, guiding them easily downstream with only occasional movements of his long steering pole.

Becky was not in sight, and John hoped she was sleeping. There was little to be done for the sailor at this point, and on the morrow they might all need what little rest they could manage.

After a time he rose and began to make his way aft. As he stepped past the lean-to John saw the girl's head emerge into the moonlight. He stopped and knelt beside her.

"Any change?" he asked softly.

"Not much. He is sleeping now." She paused, then said, "A short while ago he opened his eyes and started to speak, it seemed. But then he sort of shrugged and fell back, breathing kind of funny-like." The girl shook her head. "I do not like it, John. This is not a natural sleep, to my thinking. Before, it appeared he was fighting the poison, and perhaps some demons of his own besides. Now it's almost as if he has quit fighting both."

They sat together in silence for several minutes, watching the ripples on the dark water. At last John rose, but was halted by a sound within the thatched shelter. Peering inside with the girl, he saw the old sailor trying to rise from his pallet.

Becky moved back and caught his arm, speaking softly and trying to get the seaman to lie down once more. But the older man shook his head impatiently.

"No, lass." Blackie's voice was weak. "Let me look at the stars again. I've the thought I've little enough time to gaze upon them now."

She glanced at John, who had joined her at the sailor's side. The frontiersman nodded and together they helped their comrade to the entrance of the lean-to. His features were ghastly pale in the moonlight, and his face was damp with sweat. When he turned his head toward MacKenzie, his blue eyes shone with unnatural brightness.

"I lied to you once, lad," he said, smiling faintly. "I did. If you'll reach behind my belt you'll find a sort of a pocket there. Inside is a bit of a map showin' where the treasure's hid. I'd never trust my old memory with anythin' that important." His smile broadened slightly. "Be a hell of a turn to get to that island and not be able to find what I was lookin' for, wouldn't it?"

With gentle fingers, John probed the sailor's belt, removing a small square of parchment with writing on it. He held it up for Blackie to see, but did not unfold it.

"Well enough." The seaman nodded. "An' now if you'd call that slave-hunter up here, there's somethin' else I'd be wantin' to do."

MacKenzie turned and saw Jeremiah still standing at his post, his eyes focused on the far shore. He was clearly trying to avoid listening, though he could not help but overhear a part of what was being said only a few feet away. John rose and approached the black man, who handed over his pole and strode slowly forward.

Blackie looked up as he drew near. "This here's the speakin' of my last will and testament," he said. "I've no people o' my own. Never did have. But you pulled me from the water and you tried to save my life. You've taken it on yourself to share in our fightin' and our troubles. No kin could do more, to my way o' thinkin'.

"So Jeremiah I, Robert Teague, do now name you

my sole heir and assign, heir to one third o' that which lies buried at the end o' this river. One third of a fortune in pirate gold!" He took a deep breath, still fixing the other man's eyes with his own.

"But on one condition," he said grimly. "An' that is that you stay clear o' this slavin' business from now on. I've done things in my day that I'm not so proud of, but even I never held no other human bein's in bondage. And I won't have my heir doin' it neither." He glanced at John and Becky. "Now if you agree, say so before these witnesses. And we'll consider the matter settled."

Jeremiah held the older man's gaze. "I agree," he said quietly, "without no regrets at all." Then he added more softly, "And I thank you, Blackie Teague."

The sailor only nodded. Then he raised his eyes to the star-filled sky and it was several minutes before he spoke again. "My life is done," he said at last. "I feel it, I feel the coldness upon me. 'Twas not so much to show for forty-seven years after all. But I've the feelin' I'm leavin' somethin' behind me now, in better hands than my own, to . . ."

He did not finish the sentence, and after a moment John looked down at his comrade. The blue eyes were still open, gazing blindly up at the moon and the stars. And there was a faint smile on the old sailor's face.

They buried Blackie on a bluff overlooking the river, where his spirit could watch the gentle current as it flowed steadily down to the sea. It was slow work in the moonlight, but the men took their time and did the job well, for both felt their friend deserved no less.

When they were finished and MacKenzie had spoken a few simple words over the grave, dawn was only an hour or two away.

17

THEY RETURNED TO THE RAFT quickly, boarding and pressing on without delay, for still there was the danger of pursuit. The sooner they reached their destination and left this broad waterway, the sooner they might avoid or lessen that danger.

The sun was high in the sky and the day had become sweltering in the absence of even the slightest hint of a breeze when they rounded yet another bend of the river's serpentine course and saw a low bluff dead ahead. It seemed to make up a fair-sized expanse of dry land where the river curved past it to the right, and then back to the left again.

The banks here alternated between dense hardwood hammocks and marshy grasslands, cut through by hundreds of creeks and narrow rivulets. The San Juanito itself was growing wider, and the current was slowing accordingly. It was near midday now, and John guessed that they had still some seven or eight hours of travel ahead of them.

He considered the possibility of going ashore for a nooning. They had been on the water constantly since yesterday morning, with their only landing being the night before when they had buried their friend. A meal of fresh game and a few hours' rest in the cool shade of the oaks and hickories that lined the river was an appealing thought. The lost time mattered less now, for they could not hope to reach their destination before nightfall in any case.

Standing at the back of the raft, sculling slowly with the pole, MacKenzie studied the higher ground ahead of them. From his present vantage point he could see no easy approach to it across the watery savannahs that separated it from the forest a mile or so away. The position should be reasonably defensible, in case that need should arise.

He drew nearer to the shore, searching with his eyes for a likely landing place. Then suddenly, for no reason he could explain, John steered the raft away and back into the current. Perhaps he wished to avoid this side of the bluff, as being too easily visible from a boat or canoe coming downriver. Perhaps it was simply a habit of caution, formed long ago, that made him uneasy about putting in at the most obvious spot.

He was aware of no such rational process as he poled away from the bank and swung the craft to his right, then back to the left a few minutes later, rounding the point. His reaction had been instinctive, almost automatic.

A word to Becky and Jeremiah earlier had prepared them for a landing, so both were now kneeling at the edge of the raft ready to take hold of roots or overhanging branches and draw them ashore once John had chosen the place. Now he saw a low sandy beach, sheltered by the limbs of several trees. He began steering toward it.

A heron wading in the shallows lifted its head from the water curiously. But instead of eyeing the approaching raft as might be expected, the bird's attention was drawn to the dark shadows of the shoreline behind it.

Instantly John dug his pole into the mud and leaned hard upon it to propel them back into the swifter current at the center of the river. As he did so he thought he saw a brief glint of sunlight on metal.

He was forced to bend over suddenly in order not to lose the pole to the mire of the soft river bottom. For some reason he glanced at Jeremiah and saw the other man start to pick up his rifle. There was a tremendous blow at the back of John's head and he felt himself falling. Then everything went black.

MacKenzie woke to the agony of throbbing pain behind his ears. It was some time before he could get his bearings or remember where he was. When he opened his eyes at last, his vision was blurred. And when he tried to shake his head to clear it the pain shot downward through his body like red-hot daggers, so that he was forced to lie still for many minutes afterward, fighting back the vertigo and gasping for breath.

Gradually it came to him that he was in the water, lying with his arms across a driftwood log in the shallows of the river. Somehow, without ever becoming fully conscious, he had managed to rise to the surface and take hold of the piece of flotsam that had saved his life. He had no memory whatever of doing so.

It was obvious he had a concussion. The blurred vision would have told him that even without the throbbing torment at the back of his skull. He lay still for a long time, lapsing in and out of consciousness, too weak even to draw himself ashore.

After an endless time John opened his eyes and saw that his vision was beginning to clear. Soon he was aware enough of his surroundings to glance up at the sun. It was almost resting on the treetops. He had been lying there for hours, and the raft was nowhere in sight.

Vaguely he recalled the sound of a shot as he was

falling into the water. Raising a hand gingerly to his head, John felt the hair matted with blood. The wound seemed not to be a serious one, but he could feel a slight groove in the back of his skull. It had been a near thing. If he had not bent over suddenly to pull the boat pole from the mud, he would be dead now.

He'd no idea what had happened to Becky and Jeremiah. He could only hope that they had managed to stay with the raft and float downstream out of danger. The attacker might follow them, for there was no concealing their route along this broad waterway, but if they could keep moving until nightfall they might escape for the time being. At any rate John could take comfort in the fact that the girl's companion was a fighting man. She would be as safe with Jeremiah as anyone.

At the moment there seemed to be no help for MacKenzie aside from his own skill and determination. The situation was not new to him. All that was needed was to decide what to do, and then to make a beginning.

He raised his head a few inches and looked around. The water was glassy calm in the late afternoon. There was no sign of his attacker. There was no sign of any human presence at all, no matter where John looked. He studied his surroundings for a long time, making sure.

At last he gave a thought to moving. Though normally a strong swimmer, he knew he was too weak now from loss of blood and the shock of his wound to make it very far in the water, nor on land either for that matter. He gently rocked the log where he rested, decided it would float, and that it would probably support his weight as well. Nor did it seem to be too seriously entangled among the roots of the shoreline to be dislodged.

Rolling onto his side he brought his knees up to place his feet against the shallow river bottom. He grasped the log more firmly, then pushed out hard with his legs. There was a sudden shooting pain at the base of John's skull. He closed his eyes against it, and lay still for several minutes.

The log had moved, though only slightly. After a time he tried again. Slowly, painfully, through repeated efforts and frequent pauses to rest, he at last got it free from the bank and into the current. When he felt himself floating downstream he closed his eyes and breathed deeply, entirely drained by his exertions.

How long he traveled, or how far, he had no idea. Sometimes he lost consciousness, and woke to find himself aground where the river curved around a low bank or a thick stand of cypress. Each time there was another painful struggle to break free and push himself back into the current. Each time he felt the effort had sapped his last reserves of strength. But somehow he found the means to keep going.

The light was fading when he woke once more to find himself aground on the narrow sandy beach of an island in the middle of the river. He looked carefully around him in the gathering twilight, realizing that it made little sense to continue his journey after dark. It was difficult enough to navigate the bends and shallows of the river by day in his present condition. And he needed sleep badly.

He hoped his friends were safe, but if they were in need of help he'd little to offer at the moment in any case. And night was the hunting time of alligators and many other predators. It was best to find some safe haven now, where he could rest and conserve his strength for the morrow.

The island where he lay was perhaps two hundred yards wide by a quarter of a mile long. It seemed strangely barren of undergrowth, but there were trees which might offer a certain measure of safety. Some of them had low branches that would make climbing easy even for a man in John's current condition.

Painfully he began the job of dragging himself ashore, rolling over and crawling on his elbows until he was well out of the water. He rested, and then with a supreme effort, managed to get his legs under him and stand up. Stumbling clumsily, he made his way to a water oak some fifty feet away. There he fell to his knees and bent his head forward against his chest for several long minutes, breathing in deep, ragged gasps.

At last he looked up. The lowest limb was perhaps seven feet from the ground. He placed his arms around the bole of the tree and slowly pulled himself erect. After another pause to catch his breath, he managed to raise his hands and take hold of the limb over his head.

How he made it up to that limb, and beyond it to another, and still another, John could not say. But finally he found himself in a kind of natural bower where several branches met to form a sturdy support some twelve feet off the ground. With fumbling fingers he undid his belt and used it to fasten himself securely in place. Exhausted, he fell asleep almost instantly.

He woke to a raging thirst, no doubt brought on by his earlier loss of blood. John lay still for some time however, taking stock and listening to the silence of the night. He was terribly weak, but the rest had already done him good. His years of hard living in the wilderness had given his body resilience as well as strength.

The moon was almost full, and he could see the branches overhead in sharp relief. It was one of those clear tropical nights when the moon cast deep shadows, and a man could see almost as well by its light as he could by day. John's ears were attuned to any sound of movement nearby, but the forest seemed uncommonly still at this hour.

Carefully loosening the belt that held him in place, he rolled over slightly and looked down. The tree was in the middle of a clearing some thirty yards in diameter, bordered by the still waters of the San Juanito on the north and the east. John could see clearly in every direction. Nothing seemed to be stirring.

Turning his head, he studied the river bank and the rippling water beyond for perhaps fifteen minutes, taking his time, wanting to miss nothing. He needed a drink badly, but had no intention of coming upon any roving predators unawares — neither feline, reptilian, nor human.

At last, satisfied that there was nothing out of the ordinary within his range of vision, he took hold of the branches and began to descend, moving cautiously and silently from long habit. When he reached the ground he found it necessary to pause and catch his breath. Again he studied his surroundings.

Seeing nothing, he crossed the open space to the river on legs grown rubbery as a result of his weakness and the hours of awkward rest among the tree limbs. With another glance all around, he lay down on the sandy bank.

He drank deeply, rested, and then drank again. Before lowering his head a third time he paused to listen once more, curious. He was struck by the odd stillness of the night. What few forest sounds he heard seemed distant, far removed from this location.

Rising at last from the river bank, he started back toward the safety of his tree. But when he was a dozen feet away he froze suddenly in his tracks. There was something close by, some animal rustling and snuffling among the leaves in the shadows across the clearing. John stayed where he was, unmoving but with every sense alert.

The noise came again. Then it was echoed, somewhere off to his left, by a second creature. And again on his right, yet more distant this time.

John thought he saw gray forms moving ghostlike

through the forest in the distance. He shuddered momentarily, then slowly resumed his approach to the tree, placing each foot with care so as to make as little sound as possible.

When he was perhaps five feet from the lowest limb a huge head appeared suddenly from the sparse undergrowth in front of him. Its tiny close-set eyes stared directly into his. Behind the ugly snout four razor-sharp tusks gleamed yellowly in the moonlight.

John's knife had found its way into his hand by reflex, but he knew there was little chance he could survive even the first charge of the three-hundred-pound boar. It took a brave man to face even one of these fierce creatures with a rifle and specially trained dogs. And from the sounds coming now from every quarter, MacKenzie knew that he was in the midst of a sizable pack.

He glanced at the nearest limb, gauging his chances. His weakness was forgotten now, for if he failed to reach the safety of the tree he would be cut to ribbons in an instant by the creature's tusks. In minutes the boar and his companions would have left nothing behind but a few crushed bones.

The animal took three or four mincing steps forward, preparatory to charging. There was no time left. Thrusting the knife back in his belt, John took a quick stride, planted his feet, and jumped.

His hands caught and he followed through with his forward motion, swinging his legs up and then over the branch. The skin of his palms was shredded by the rough bark as this hands turned with his body's movement. Clinging desperately to the limb, John felt the boar's massive body collide with the tree trunk, shaking it to its very roots.

The creature grunted fiercely and backed off, shaking its head and eyeing the oak as if considering yet another charge against this stubborn enemy. John scrambled higher and saw several of the boar's companions gathering in the open nearby, drawn by the sound of the attack. Their tusks were bloody. Somewhere on this barren island they must have surprised a hapless family of opossums or other small game not very long before.

More nocturnal quarry had been run to ground as well, for everywhere now MacKenzie could hear the grunts and roars of the wild hogs in their feeding frenzy, together with the frantic squealing of a dozen or more young shoats. On every side the small island was a cacophony of furious sound.

He found a high perch and clung there, watching in fascination while the savage creatures moved to and fro below him in the moonlight. John was safe enough for the moment. But he had heard of men treed for hours, even days, by such a pack. The sparse undergrowth meant the beasts had been on the island for some time now, and it might be another long while before they decided to leave.

After several minutes he tore his eyes away to clean and wrap his bloody hands with the kerchief from his neck. Then, situating himself as comfortably as possible in the crotch of two limbs, he fastened his belt about the branches once more. He tried to compose himself for sleep, but the noises below seemed to abate only slightly as the minutes passed, and he found it impossible to ignore them. Shifting his body slightly, John looked down again at the clearing.

The wild hogs were still milling about, rooting through the leaves and earth now for pine cones and similar forage. Apparently there was no more live game to be found in the immediate vicinity. From time to time the old boar glanced at John's tree, as if vaguely recalling that there was still one prospect of fresh meat nearby, if only he could figure out how to get to it.

MacKenzie's eyes were suddenly drawn to the tip of the island, where the dark water flowed silently past on either side. There seemed to be a large log on the bank that had not been there earlier. He studied it thoughtfully, then moved his gaze in a circle around the shadowed perimeter of the clearing.

He saw two bright points of light appear, burning like fiery coals for an instant before returning to darkness. A moment later a second pair winked on and off a few yards away, this time greenish yellow in the moonlight. As his eyes scanned the shadows beneath the trees John could make out other pairs of lights, twinkling evilly like fallen stars. He counted eight pairs in all.

A few minutes later he watched a rough body rise on short curved legs and waddle closer to the unsuspecting hogs in the clearing. It moved quickly, more quickly than seemed possible for such an ungainly shape. Yet it was stealthy and silent as a stalking panther. Soon the other alligators began to advance, leap-frogging rapidly ahead of one another in order to draw the deadly circle ever tighter around their prey.

A shoat near the edge of the pack looked up suddenly and squealed a warning. The big boar raised its massive head. But it was too late. The trap was sprung.

The shoat disappeared in an instant, not even a proper mouthful for the nine-foot female that had been stalking it. The other gators were attacking too, their fearsome jaws gaping briefly in the moonlight before snapping audibly shut to grind their quarry to pieces between row upon row of razor-sharp teeth. John recalled hearing from an old Indian that pork was these prehistoric monsters' favorite meat.

The big boar had started toward the forest at the first signs of attack, but had found its way blocked at every turn. It began circling the clearing, snorting and swinging its head from side to side in vexation, seemingly oblivious to the bloody fate of its comrades.

Suddenly it spun half around and charged blindly into the gap between two female alligators who had just finished dispatching a pair of sows. The closest gator caught the boar with a vicious swipe of her tail, knocking it on its side and into her companion. Slashing wildly upward with his tusks, the boar ripped a gaping hole in the female's throat.

It was to be his final revenge however, for an instant

later his hindquarters were caught fast in the saurian's crushing jaws. With a horrible squealing bellow, accompanied by the fierce booming of a bull gator on the other side of the clearing, the massive head disappeared into the second gator's gaping maw.

MacKenzie tore his eyes from this scene of slaughter with an involuntary shudder. After a few minutes he realized that all the other hogs — any that were not yet dead — had disappeared from view. The clearing was a bloody shambles. John had seen fighting and killing in his time, but nothing like the shocking carnage of this past half hour. It was enough to last a man a lifetime.

The wounded female alligator had begun making her way slowly and painfully toward the river, leaving a trail of gore behind her which shone bright in the moonlight. When he saw the other gators fall in behind her with their tip-toed stalking gait, MacKenzie closed his eyes with a sigh and rolled over so that his face was toward the heavens.

At long last the sounds of battle and feeding died away completely, and the forest was still once more. John lay staring up at the moonlit branches overhead for many minutes, watching their gentle movements in the faint evening breeze

18 🌴

Dawn came gently to the narrow island in the San Juanito, carrying no hint in its damp coolness of the raging passions of the night before. MacKenzie slept until the sun rose above the tree tops and turned their points to golden lances in its burnishing light. It was no chill in the air which made him shiver slightly as his eyes finally opened.

After a few minutes he untied himself from his perch, rolled over and climbed cautiously to the ground.

The island and the forest seemed silent and deserted now. John gritted his teeth as he set foot on the slippery earth, strewn as far as the eye could see with the bloody remnants of the battle and the frenzied moonlight feast.

After a look in all directions, he started south along the narrow beach that bordered the island. He wanted a drink badly, but had no desire to remain in this spot even for the briefest of times. He would walk to the far end of the island first.

The activity quickly worked the kinks from his limbs, and he found he was beginning to feel almost recovered from his wound. There was some weakness still, and the constant thirst to remind him of his loss of blood. But in general his body seemed fit enough, and ready for whatever lay ahead.

In a few minutes he came in sight of the southern tip of the island. He knelt among some reeds and paused to study the river and the forest beyond. The water was glassy calm in the morning light, with only thin wisps of fog still hugging the fringes of the tree-lined shore. Except for an occasional bird in flight, there seemed to be no sign at all of the abundant life he knew to be about him on every side.

Flattening himself beside the still water he drank deeply, then drank again. As he rose to his knees at last, a distant movement downriver caught his eye. Holding perfectly still, John waited and watched while a dark object rounded the bend a half mile off and drew gradually closer. He soon recognized the raft, and then the dusky figure of Jeremiah, poling with steady deliberate movements upstream against the current.

MacKenzie remained where he was, seeing no reason to expose himself fully until his friends were close by. When the raft was perhaps fifty feet away, he rose from the reeds and lifted a hand. Jeremiah saw him instantly, and began turning the craft in toward the island, bringing it to shore only a few yards from where John stood.

"It's that glad I am to see you here," the black man said as they met and clasped hands on the narrow bank. A brief smile crossed his lips, but his eyes and his voice were grave.

"And I as well," John said, "for I'd no idea at all how I might continue from here. . . ." He paused, studying the other's manner. Before he could ask the question, however, the Negro spoke again:

"It's the lass," he said quickly. "She's been taken. An' I'm afraid it's my fault entirely!"

"Taken?" A sudden fear clutched at MacKenzie's vitals. "Taken how? When? By whom?"

"This mornin' on the river, not more'n a hour ago or so. We'd just put out from the shore where we'd tied up for the night, when LeBeau appeared suddenly from the water beside us. He took hold o' the girl and pulled her in with him, then made off for the far shore. I couldn't risk no shot for fear o' hittin' her, an' — " the black man paused and shook his head — "I reckon I just never was much for swimmin'. Never managed to rightly learn how."

John's face was grim, but he placed a hand gently on the other man's shoulder. "What's done is done," he said. "An' frettin' over it will not undo it, nor will blamin' yourself for what could not be helped." He strode to the raft. "Come on, do you show me the place where you last saw them. We must pick up their trail without delay!"

He paused only long enough to find two loaded pistols and shove them into his belt. Then he lifted one of the long poles and thrust it into the water. Jeremiah was on the other side of the raft now, already pushing off from shore. With both men poling with the current, it took very little time to reach the place on the east bank where LeBeau and the girl had disappeared.

The half-breed's trail was clear enough, for the big man had been moving fast. A short distance inland they found where his horse had been tied. Here there had been a brief struggle, but Becky had apparently been quickly subdued. They were mounted double now, traveling rapidly toward the northeast and parallel to the river.

MacKenzie and Jeremiah shared few words as they read these signs and started in pursuit. Both knew that they would need all their breath for the distance ahead. A man on foot could always run down a mounted man in time. But time was their enemy in the present circumstances. LeBeau was a beast, known to have little regard for the gentler sex except as an object to satisfy his brutal appetites!

John and the black man ran side by side for half a

mile, then walked, then ran again, holding to a pace men of their hardened condition were able to maintain for hours if need be. They had no way of knowing yet if they were gaining or losing ground. But the horse's tracks in the dew-wet earth remained fresh, so there was still hope.

The day was growing hot, and as they advanced John loosened the ties of his buckskin jacket, then removed it and thrust it behind his belt. His earlier weakness was forgotten. His only thought was of the girl and her brutal captor ahead, and of the urgent need for haste.

After two hours MacKenzie halted suddenly and knelt to study the ground. He glanced up at Jeremiah as the other man drew abreast.

"Horse stumbled," John said, speaking between deep breaths, "and not the first time. Without stops an' carryin' double, it could be close to played out. I've a feelin' the man's no respecter of horseflesh, as well as of women." The other man nodded silently, bending over to rest with his hands upon his knees.

After a brief pause they resumed the chase. A mile farther on they found the horse, lying beside the trail and gasping its last. John glanced warily around him at the silent forest, then knelt to study the sign.

"They're afoot now," he said, his voice low. "And no more than an hour ahead is my guess." He glanced at his companion.

Jeremiah knelt beside the frontiersman. "Aye," he

said. "I don't 'magine he'll run much farther now. Not his style. Tried to get away, but didn't make it. Now he'll fight. Likely be layin' for us somewheres up ahead."

John agreed. He sat back on his heels, his brow furrowed in thought. They were still close to the San Juanito, and their route had led them into a country of low wooded ridges thrown up by the periodic flooding of the river, and separated by deep gullies. Dead trees and blowdowns were everywhere, killed by the rising waters or by wildfires sometime in the past. It was treacherous country, well-suited for an ambush. They could not afford to risk blundering into a trap at this stage of the game.

After a moment he spoke a few words to Jeremiah and the two separated, moving silently through the tangled terrain on either side of the trail. They would advance in a wide arc, converging again after a time on the route before them and scouting the country between in the meantime. The process could be repeated as often as necessary, until one or the other of them sighted their quarry.

It was a calculated gamble, for such an approach would take time and if they had misjudged LeBeau's intentions the half-breed could be miles away before that fact was discovered. But on foot and with an unwilling prisoner, his pace would be slowed. And no man, regardless of his skills, could conceal his trail from a knowing tracker for long.

Unless, John thought grimly, he had a boat or a

canoe hidden somewhere nearby. But that was a chance they had to take. For to risk ambush by LeBeau was to risk leaving Becky to his mercy permanently.

MacKenzie advanced cautiously through the eerie landscape of decaying leaves, lichen-crusted stumps and ghostly skeletons of dead trees. His eyes moved steadily, left to right, ground to sky and back again, missing nothing.

He kept to low ground, careful to avoid skylining himself on one of the sand ridges. From time to time he paused and knelt to crawl warily up an embankment, using blowdowns or standing trees at the top for concealment as he searched the surrounding terrain.

He saw nothing, heard nothing. Even the birds and insects seemed strangely still in this place, as if they too shared the frontiersman's impending sense of danger.

When he had gone perhaps a thousand yards he realized it was time to turn in once more toward his next planned meeting with Jeremiah. Each step had increased John's uneasiness and his caution, for he somehow felt certain that the big half-breed was lying in wait nearby, his rifle poised and ready in an instant to reduce the odds against himself by half.

A successful hunter needs to understand his quarry, and MacKenzie felt he knew LeBeau well enough by now. The man was like a wild beast, a predator. Such creatures might at first try to avoid combat, but if flight became impossible it was in their nature to meet their enemy head-on, with all the savage strength and fury at their command. At such a time they would be ready to kill or be killed without the slightest hesitation.

After moving forward another hundred yards John paused to consider his route. In order to advance in the direction he wanted to go, he would have to cross the low wooded ridge immediately before him.

A short distance away he saw the huge hollowed-out trunk of a dead cypress. It would provide good cover for his approach up the rise. Beyond that a tangle of young blackjack and hickory on the crest would provide at least partial concealment for his crossing. He would be exposed briefly in moving from one to the other, but still it seemed as likely a spot as any.

Stepping forward in a crouch until he was at the base of the tree, MacKenzie dropped to his knees and held still for a long moment, listening intently before starting upward. He heard nothing but the occasional rustle of leaves in the wind off the river. To a frontiersman the sound was easily distinguished from the movements of birds, animals or men, and he discounted it in the same instant that it reached his awareness.

Placing each hand and knee with care and pressing down lightly on the leafy carpet before inching his body forward, John began to climb the rise. He was in no hurry. Silent movement in the forest took time, but it was his greatest protection. Lack of patience in the face of any hidden danger could easily get a man killed.

When he was near the top of the embankment he carefully lifted his head a few inches adjacent to the fluted trunk. Taking his time, he scanned the ground beyond. Everything about him in these shadowed woodlands appeared as still and silent as the tomb.

He lowered his head and, moving with infinite care to the opposite side of the tree, repeated the process. Still he saw nothing. At last he started upward, inching forward on his belly toward the hardwood thicket some dozen yards away.

Upon reaching it after what seemed an endless time, he lay still and took several slow, easy breaths. Once inside the low thicket he could make his way to the other side in relative secrecy, though he must take particular care not to disturb any of the branches as he moved.

He lifted his head slightly to take one final look around before continuing on.

The crash of a rifle shot shattered the forest stillness, and John instantly dropped flat onto the leaves and moist earth. A second later another shot boomed, clipping a twig directly over his head.

"Missed him!" It was Jeremiah's voice. "May be I spoilt his aim a bit, anyhow. If you can hear me, Mackenzie, look out! He'll be comin' your way now!"

John knew he was spotted, and to move at all was to offer a larger target. From his present position he could neither reach his weapons nor withdraw without raising up. He decided to take a chance. If LeBeau was moving himself just then, he might have no opportunity to take careful aim.

Rolling over quickly three times, John slid down the

reverse slope of the ridge a bare instant before a pistol ball sprayed sand and leaves from his earlier position. He heard a sharp curse in French.

Drawing both his pistols, MacKenzie came to his knees at the bottom of the ravine. He wasted a shot as the hulking half-breed appeared briefly on the crest of the ridge, then used the seconds gained while the other hit the ground to retreat a dozen yards to the partial cover of a rotting tree stump. He had one shot left now. LeBeau likely had no more than that, and perhaps he had already used his last one. Neither man could afford the time to reload.

A noise brought John around suddenly and his pistol came up as the big man appeared from behind a tree some twenty yards away. He pulled the trigger and the hammer sprang forward with a harmless click!

John's rapid movements must have dislodged the priming load, or perhaps the powder had suffered from the moist climate. It mattered little, for the shot had failed and the big half-breed was advancing now with a knife low in his right hand. Discarding the useless pistol, MacKenzie rose quickly into a crouch and drew his own blade.

If the fight with Ben Pike two days ago had been decided by cunning and finesse, John saw immediately that this one was far more likely to be resolved by brute force alone. LeBeau was a huge man, outweighing his smaller opponent by easily fifty pounds, and with the advantage in height and reach as well. The muscles of the half-breed's arms and shoulders bulged the fabric of his linen shirt as he flexed them while circling warily, his eyes searching for an opening.

They tested each other with several tentative thrusts and feints, not so much calculated to do damage to an opponent as to uncover his style of fighting and his possible weaknesses. John could readily see that his enemy was no novice, but he was perhaps a trifle too anxious to seek an advantage, to close and finish the battle quickly. The reason was clear enough: Jeremiah could not be far away at this moment, and LeBeau had no desire to face two enemies at once.

Taking this as his cue John played for time, avoiding the other man's attempts to close and backing slowly off across the leaf-covered clearing. But soon he found himself against the trunk of a large cypress which blocked his retreat temporarily. LeBeau saw and reacted in an instant, advancing, dropping his knife hand, and slashing savagely upward in a single movement.

MacKenzie leapt to one side, avoiding disembowelment by a fraction of an inch. He threw himself against the big man's arm as the knife embedded itself deeply in the wood. The blow was a lucky one, as well as powerful, and the half-breed's blade snapped cleanly off at the hilt.

But the sudden movement had thrown John off balance, and as he sought to recover LeBeau struck him hard across the face with the back of one hand, then managed to close the fingers of the other tightly around his foe's knife wrist. The half-breed's grip was like steel, and his dirty fingernails dug hard into the skin of Mac-Kenzie's forearm.

A vicious blow to the midsection followed by a savage twist of the wrist forced the blade from John's numbing fingers. As he let it go he turned and brought a knee up sharply, aimed at the other man's groin. LeBeau blocked the move by twisting quickly away, but he could not avoid a follow-up left hook to the jaw with all of John's strength behind it.

More surprised than hurt, the big man blinked and released his grip on MacKenzie's arm. He aimed another vicious backhand at his smaller opponent's head, and the blow connected.

Brilliant lights flashed suddenly before John's eyes. He hit the ground and rolled, coming up fast to see his foe advancing with a leather-soled boot poised to stomp the life out of him.

Sidestepping, MacKenzie grabbed hold of the leg firmly and stood up. LeBeau fell backward, hit the ground, and rolled over quickly, drawing both legs up to his chest. When John tried to move in he was met with a wild kick that threw him back a dozen yards to the forest floor.

Both men rose from the ground more slowly now, and again they began to circle warily.

19

SUDDENLY THE HALF-BREED CAME IN, fast and low, a savage grin on his face and his arms spread wide. He met John's elbow at the end of his lunge, hard across the cheek-bone and then back again. But these blows seemed scarcely to faze him. Grasping MacKenzie's waist with his right arm he placed his left hand beneath the other's chin, pushing his opponent's head back while his fingers reached out, seeking the nose and eyes.

John stamped down hard on LeBeau's instep, then twisted quickly away as the other howled in pain. Turning full around, he used the momentum of this movement to follow through with a vicious right to the jaw, and then a left to the wind and a right uppercut with all of his strength behind it to the half-breed's solar plexus.

LeBeau backed away a step gasping for breath, and John followed him in, showing no mercy. The pain of his earlier hurts had awakened the fighter in MacKenzie, and he scarcely felt the blows the big man threw now as he furiously tried to ward off the Scotsman's attack.

John landed a hard right over the heart, then a left to the same place, followed by a sweeping right to the jaw. Thrusting a thumb into each ear he pulled the half-breed's head down to his own in a "Liverpool Kiss" that broke LeBeau's nose and showered both men with blood.

The big man's hands were clutching blindly for John's throat, but John ignored them and tightened his grip on his enemy's ears. Then he brought the head down sharply once more to meet his upraised knee.

It was a blow that would have finished a lesser man. But LeBeau shook it off and remained standing, moving his head groggily from side to side and spraying huge drops of blood from his pulped nose onto the brown leaves at his feet. One eye was swollen shut, and yellow teeth leered grotesquely at John through an ugly cut in the half-breed's lower lip.

He stood where he was briefly as MacKenzie backed

away, then launched himself in a low stumbling dive that caught the smaller man around the hips and threw him violently backward. John had no choice but to let himself go with the movement, landing hard on his shoulders. Somehow he managed to get his knees up and use the half-breed's momentum to throw him over his head to the ground a dozen feet away. But the move had knocked John's breath from him, and he was slow to rise and turn around.

LeBeau had taken hold of a huge tree limb, and as John turned he saw a vicious roundhouse blow coming directly at his head. There was no time to think. He threw himself to the ground and the limb missed decapitating him by inches.

MacKenzie caught a glint of metal as he fell, and almost without thinking his fingers reached out and closed around the hilt of his knife, dropped there minutes before. He rolled over and came to his knees, gasping for breath and holding the blade out before him with both hands.

The half-breed started forward again brandishing the tree limb, but halted when he saw the knife. He stood for a long moment on swaying legs, shaking his massive head ponderously from side to side as more drops of blood spattered the leaves of the clearing. Then the big man grinned suddenly through his shredded lips, fixed John balefully with his good eye, and started forward.

MacKenzie saw his intention in an instant, and almost without thinking opened his mouth to warn him off. But his words were drowned out by a guttural roar from LeBeau as the half-breed dropped the limb and rushed forward. His fingers closed around MacKenzie's throat at the same instant that the blade sank to the hilt in the soft flesh of his huge belly.

John felt his windpipe being crushed slowly, inexorably, in the dying man's viselike grip. He twisted his head and fought for breath, but dared not let go of the knife. Instead he thrust it upward with all his might, twisting with both hands, then brought the blade down again in a full circle that gouged a great gaping path through his enemy's vitals. Still the iron-hard fingers continued their relentless pressure at his throat. John felt himself becoming light-headed. He closed his eyes briefly against the pain.

When he opened them again LeBeau was staring into his face, his mouth working awkwardly. But no words came.

Then slowly, mercifully, MacKenzie felt the other man's fingers begin to relax their grip. The half-breed rose in one final convulsive shudder, and rolled slowly over onto his side.

John remained where he was for a long time, kneeling on the soft earth and gasping harshly for breath. For some reason he could not seem to take his eyes from the bloody knife in his hands. Finally his fingers opened and he let the blade drop. A moment later he fell backward onto the leaves of the clearing, drained emotionally as well as physically by his ordeal.

After a while he felt a cool hand touch his forehead, and looked up to see Becky on her knees beside him. Jeremiah was standing nearby with a concerned look on his face, but when he saw John's eyes open he smiled broadly.

"I reckon you done it, lad. An' without that much help from me, neither." The black man nodded toward Becky. "I couldn't leave the lass back there where I found her, all trussed up like a turkey ready for Thanksgivin' dinner. But when I'd set her free an' we finally made it over here, you'd already done made an end to it all."

John nodded and tried to answer, but his voice wouldn't come. His throat hurt terribly, and he was still having some trouble catching his breath. He met the girl's eyes once more, and felt consciousness slipping away from him.

When next he woke Becky was gently working to clean the cuts and bruises on his face with a moist cloth. From the position of the sun it seemed that John had been unconscious for perhaps an hour.

The body of LeBeau was gone now, and Jeremiah was seated on the trunk of a fallen pine tree a few feet away, cleaning and recharging their weapons. When he saw MacKenzie open his eyes the black man grinned and set the long rifle he'd been working on upright against the trunk.

"Right fine piece that," he said. "Lass tells me 'twas yours at the time all this started." He indicated the array of firearms laid out on the rough bark beside him. "Seems we've enough weapons to start a armory now, what with the half-breed's an' all them we brought with us. Might even spare one for the lass here — if she knew what to do with it."

Becky continued her ministrations without looking up.

"I might surprise you," she said calmly. "I'd a father and five brothers at home, and an uncle with the King's Highlanders. As it turns out I've been shooting ever since I was a girl, with shotgun, fusee" — she glanced at the black man — "and with pistols, too."

"Y' might have told us that," MacKenzie said with a good-natured grin. "'Twould 'a saved a deal o' trouble an' worry if we'd known. We could 'a simply armed you at the start of all this, an' then let you go ahead an' fend for yourself!"

"Aye." She nodded. "It might at that. For had I been able to lay my hands on a weapon when that brute took me, I'd have done for him sure enough! And I might have tried anyway, with his own pistol. But he bound me hand and foot, then threw me across his horse like a sack of grain." She shook her head. "'Twas a most unladylike way to travel!"

Jeremiah rose and stretched, then looked down at John.

"Speakin' o' travel," he said, "D'you think you might feel up to another few hours now? We could make camp right here if need be, but all our provisions an' such are back at the raft." He glanced at the sun. "An' we ought to just about make it there by nightfall, if we start right away."

They made camp at twilight, in a small hollow among a stand of oak and black gum not far from the water's edge. It was a place carefully chosen so that their fire would be invisible from any point upon the river or its banks.

To their knowledge there were no more pursuers nearby, but caution was a habit neither MacKenzie nor Jeremiah was inclined to break. Both believed it foolish to take any risk that could be avoided, and it was a foolish man indeed who never prepared for the unexpected.

John had agreed to chance an evening fire, however. The small risk of it being seen by some person or persons unknown was more than overbalanced by the protection it could afford against predators. And the savage events of the previous night remained vividly current in his mind.

This night passed quietly though, and MacKenzie slept well for the first time in days, waking only occasionally through the dark hours to add fresh wood to the fire. They'd seen little need to set a watch now, especially as both John and Jeremiah were by habit light sleepers in the wilderness.

At daylight they breakfasted on bacon, fresh fish and johnnycake, taking a bit of extra time and effort to treat themselves and celebrate the relief they all felt that the long days of pursuit and danger seemed to be finally over. They should arrive at their destination well before nightfall today, even after the relatively late start.

It was with a feeling almost of cheerful anticipation that the three boarded the raft and set out once again into the slow-moving current. The end of their journey was in sight, and there was the very real prospect that they might discover something akin to a pot of gold at the end of the rainbow.

The day was clear and the long hours seemed to pass easily, like the fleecy clouds that floated softly overhead against the brilliant blue canopy of the sky. The walls of jungle that enclosed the river on each side became denser as they neared the Gulf of Mexico, and the abundant life of the marshlands was everywhere in evidence. Herons, egrets and other water birds were with them constantly, and in time the travelers also began to see pelicans, gulls and an occasional soaring osprey.

When the sun was a little past its zenith John dipped a finger into the river and tasted salt. It was in the air too, so that each of them could feel the timeless presence of the sea long before they actually saw it.

But at last the shimmering expanse of the Gulf came into view, seen between low islands and ragged headlands that dotted the coast for miles in every direction. A short while later they had located the island marked on Blackie's map and an hour after that they were stepping ashore to pull the raft up onto the narrow strip of sandy beach on its northern side.

John found himself looking anxiously for the land-marks noted on the sailor's well-marked parchment, and was relieved to spy a gnarled tree on a slight rise some fifty yards away. As he identified other reference points, he breathed a silent prayer of thanks. He'd kept one final fear from his companions during all their trials to this point: the possibility that they might not be able to locate the treasure from Blackie's map as drawn.

It was only seven years since Tyrone had buried his ill-gotten booty here. But John was far more aware than the others of the tremendous changes which could occur in that short period of time. Frequent storms uprooted trees and shifted the loose sands along this coast con-stantly. And the incredible force of a hurricane had been known to change the terrain entirely, sometimes creating new islands or sinking existing ones forever beneath its pounding waves.

There were two or three hours of daylight left when they made landfall, and the travelers had no desire to wait another night to see what, if anything, might lie hidden beneath the dunes and low brush at the center of the island. Each of them was anxious to bring their quest to a conclusion now, even if the final discovery brought only disappointment.

They set about their search without delay, and John found he had little trouble following Blackie's scrupu-lously recorded directions. In another hour they had located the spot indicated on the map, and quickly fetched shovels from the raft to begin their digging.

It was not an easy task, for the loose grains tried to refill the hole almost as soon as they were shoveled aside. In minutes both men were dripping with sweat as they labored under the hot afternoon sun.

The pirates could not have buried the treasure too deeply however, because of the high water table in these coastal areas. When John and Jeremiah had gone down no more than three or four feet the sand was already damp. Shortly afterward their shovels struck the lid of a sturdy metal box.

It was not overly large, but its weight seemed promising when the two men lifted it from the excavation and set it on the ground nearby. Climbing to the surface, MacKenzie wiped his forehead with the tail of his shirt and knelt to study their find.

The box was of iron, well-made and securely locked. But seven years of contact with the salt and humidity of this coast had taken their toll, and the hinges were seriously weakened by rust. Using one of the shovels as a prize, John and Jeremiah quickly managed to break both metal straps and lift the lid. The three companions looked inside.

There were a number of bundles wrapped in oil-cloth, each tied securely with string. Opening one of these, John carefully spread the cloth and its contents on the sand for all to see.

Dozens of gold and silver coins glittered in the late

afternoon sun. And two small leather sacks among the rest proved to be filled with precious gems, some cut and others uncut. When they opened more bundles, they found the contents to be equally rich. It was everything Blackie had said, and more. A fortune such as few men in this world would ever see, much less possess.

The burnished sun was low on the waters of the Gulf of Mexico, and the three friends sat in silence for a long time, gazing down at the sparkling hoard before them. It was Jeremiah who finally found words to express what each of them was feeling:

"Well," he said, shaking his head, "I reckon that old salt knew what he was talkin' about after all. Just wisht he was here to share in it. I surely do." The black man looked at his companions. "Y' know, I never did really believe in all o' this, never thought it'd be here. Not till right this minute."

John nodded. "I'd a few reservations myself," he admitted. "Even while we were diggin' I couldna quite bring myself to think it would be as the old man said. It seemed too much the stuff o' fairy tales for a practical man to put his faith in."

"I believe you've both grown a bit too 'practical' then," Becky said quietly. "'Tis all very well to prepare and be ready for the worst, but you must still believe that the good will happen sometimes." When they looked at her she was smiling. "Myself, I never doubted it for an instant!"

After a while John began wrapping the treasure into

bundles once more, replacing them carefully in the metal chest. "It's time we gave some thought to makin' camp now," he said matter-of-factly, "for the day grows late, and despite our riches we will still need rest and food. Later will be a time for countin' an' dividin' the treasure amongst ourselves."

The lilting voice at his back came across the few yards of sand with the evening breeze, low and deliberate:

"I do not think there will be any need for you to go putting yourselves to all that trouble, now. I expect we will be able to manage the finances quite well from this point forward, without your help."

Startled by the sound, MacKenzie and his companions turned quickly to discover its source. Atop a low dune a few yards away were the figures of five men, standing in silhouette against the setting sun. Their faces could not be made out with the light at their backs, but the weapons in their hands were visible enough. Nor did John have any great difficulty identifying the outline of the shorter man who was their leader.

"And besides," Tyrone added quietly, "I do not believe the three of you will find much opportunity for spending in the place where you will be going before this night is through!"

20 ☀

IN THEIR PREOCCUPATION with the treasure none of the three comrades had been aware of the men's approach over the dunes from the Gulf. Now they were trapped, and MacKenzie could see little hope of escape.

Their rifles were leaning against a tree some dozen feet away, and though John and Jeremiah each had two pistols in their belts, there was almost no chance of drawing, cocking and firing even once before they would themselves be riddled with lead. There was Becky to be considered too. The girl was kneeling on the sand only a few feet away, and the risk of her catching a stray bullet if shooting started was not one MacKenzie was prepared to take.

Tyrone advanced slowly, with his men well spread out on either side. All of them had pistols in their hands, cocked and ready to fire at the slightest sign of resistance. When the Irishman was some ten feet from John he halted, but his followers continued to move until they surrounded their captives on all sides. As the shorter man stopped before him, MacKenzie saw a coiled rawhide whip in his free hand.

"If you'll be so good as to remove your pistols and lay them on the sand before you," Tyrone said calmly, "we will proceed to the matter at hand." His lips curled in a slight smile. "One at a time if you please, and do take care to make no unnecessary movements." He indicated Jeremiah with his pistol. "You first, my lad."

"I'm not your lad," the Negro said coldly, meeting the other's eyes, "or anybody else's. But I'll do as you say, seein' I've little choice at the moment." He placed his weapons on the ground and then MacKenzie followed suit. There was nothing to be gained from resisting at this point, and each man held the slim hope that while they lived they might yet find some way to turn the situation to their advantage.

Tyrone indicated a nearby patch of open ground with a movement of his head. "Kindly rise, gentlemen, and step to your right. Very slow and easy now, until I tell you to stop."

When they had gone perhaps a dozen yards the pirate leader made Jeremiah halt and lie face downward in the sand. John was ordered to keep moving until he was some distance away. Two men kept their pistols on the black man while the others followed MacKenzie and Tyrone.

They stopped at last on a bare expanse of wind-swept beach, with the Irishman facing John a short distance away. In a single practiced motion the shorter man switched his pistol to his left hand and took the whip in his right. Then he shook out the braided rawhide to its full length on the wet sand behind him.

"I'll confess that it would please my vanity to spill your guts on a public field of honor for all to see," Tyrone said, still smiling. "But vanity's an empty thing after all, and we've little time here for the amenities." His smile broadened slightly.

"Nor is there any good reason I can see, to offer an enemy an even chance when the crown cards are all in my own hand. I will have to content myself with that little opportunity fortune has provided." Suddenly his voice turned cold. "Turn around. Now."

For the barest instant MacKenzie glanced at the pistols leveled at him. He had no doubt these men would shoot if he refused, but they meant to kill him anyway — and the others as well. As he had no intention of dying without a fight, John knew sooner or later he must take a chance.

But not quite yet, he thought, slowly turning his back on his adversary.

The first cracking blow of the whip caught him before he could get set, shredding his shirt and laying his shoulder open to the bone. John staggered, then caught himself and gritted his teeth. "'Tis a coward's way, Tyrone," he said in a low voice, "— no less than I'd expect from the likes o' . . ."

The second lash bit several inches lower. Clenching his fists until his fingernails dug into the flesh of his palms, MacKenzie forced the pain from his mind with an effort. "A coward's way," he repeated deliberately. "If you but dared to face me man-to-man, 'twould be a different story entirely!"

Again the lash was like a hot brand against John's torn and bleeding back. Tyrone spoke calmly. "Your taunts mean less than nothing to me in this place. There is no one but ourselves to know what passes here, nor any who'll ever repeat the tale."

He struck again, mercilessly, and MacKenzie suddenly hunched his shoulders against the agony, raising his hands to chest height as he did so. There was one hope, a faint one, and through the blinding pain John was determined to be ready for it, when — if — it came.

Another lance of fire bit into his back, and yet another. Then there was a slight pause as though the Irishman were taking a moment to aim his next blow.

Now! John thought. His hands went up in the same instant that the end of the rawhide began to curl about his neck. He took a firm grip, then lunged forward to pull his tormentor off balance.

Without the slightest pause, MacKenzie spun on his heels, grasped the whip and jerked hard, drawing the other man toward him even as he dove forward to meet him. Tyrone let go the lash and tried to bring his pistol to bear, but he was a fraction too slow. Seizing his wrist with steellike fingers John threw a wicked left to the midsection with every bit of his strength behind it.

He pounded a second blow to the same place, then grasped Tyrone's elbow in his left hand while pushing forward and up with his right. The Irishman yelped with pain and dropped the pistol an instant before his arm could be broken. Turning, John bent and threw the other man over his shoulder and into the air, to land on the ground a dozen feet away.

Tyrone's men had held their fire when the two came together for fear of hitting their leader. Now they had their chance, and MacKenzie braced himself for the bullets he expected to tear into his flesh at any second. But he heard only a single shot, and it came nowhere close to the place where he stood.

He looked quickly around, and saw with surprise that two of the pirates were down. One lay clutching feebly at the hilt of Jeremiah's knife where it had lodged in his belly. The other sat upright on the sand holding a bloody shoulder, smashed by a bullet from the smoking pistol in Becky's right hand.

Ignored when the fight began, the young woman had drawn the concealed weapon from her skirt and at the proper moment fired coolly into one of the men. Jeremiah had responded without hesitation, poised as he had been to take advantage of the slightest opportunity.

In another instant the girl had dropped the empty pistol and picked up another from the ground before her, cocking and aiming it in a single motion. The black man was already beside her, taking up a second weapon and turning with it to face Tyrone's remaining henchman.

Seeing how the situation had changed, and with a glance at their leader sprawled in the dirt at their feet, both pirates hesitated only briefly before letting go their weapons.

MacKenzie turned to look at the Irishman. He felt all his pent-up anger of the past two weeks slowly welling up inside of him. He'd lost a friend, been robbed, beaten, shot, and chased more than a hundred miles through the Florida wilderness with a price on his head. And the man responsible for all of that was before him now. It was the time for settling accounts.

For a moment MacKenzie hesitated, struck suddenly by the decision he had made. He wanted satisfaction from this vicious little swaggering popinjay, and he meant to have it. But without killing. There'd been too much of that already, and John had an idea it would not be needed this time.

"Get up," he said, very quietly. "Get on your feet, Dread Jamie Tyrone, and face me like a man. For before these witnesses I'm goin' to tear your temple down, an' show to all the world what a small manner o' person it is who once thought to make such a big splash in these western seas!"

The man on the ground looked up at his adversary, then glanced around the beach at the remaining members of his crew. They were all watching him intently, for the challenge was one they understood well. No leader of men could ignore such a challenge, even when given the chance to avoid it. For Tyrone it was either face Mac-Kenzie now, man-to-man, or lose whatever loyalty his crew still held for him.

Slowly he got to his feet.

And yet it was not so much a fight as a brutal and deliberate beating. Though Tyrone was game, he had never been one to face others without a weapon of some kind in his hands. The Irishman's fists proved no match at all for the iron-hard knuckles and rough fighting skill of the frontiersman. In just minutes it was over.

The pirate captain lay in a heap on the soft white sand of the island, his face a bloody pulp and his fine clothing ripped and stained from collar to toe with sweat and blood. His three surviving henchmen did not even spare a glance in his direction as they made their way across the dunes toward their waiting dinghy.

John stood with his hands on his hips, breathing easily while Tyrone rose groaning to his knees and, after another long minute, to his feet. Standing there in the sun's last rays, he swayed slightly as he glared at Mac-

Kenzie through grotesquely swollen eyes.

"It seems," John said mildly, "that your men have deserted you. And I'm afraid we've no particular desire to have you join our party either. So I reckon that you're on your own now, Dread Jamie Tyrone, to return to civilization or wherever it is you wish to go, in the best way you can manage by yourself."

He took the sheathed knife from his belt and tossed it to the other. "I'll see no man completely unarmed in the wilderness, and you can have a bit o' food from our stores as well. But then I'll ask you to leave this place, and not to show your face again in this country where it can be seen by myself or any other honest man."

John paused, then added quietly: "Y' understand, that's not a warnin' I'd be wantin' to give to you twice."

Turning, he indicated a nearby island with a wave of his hand. "'Tis no more than a thousand yards over there, and you should make that easily enough, assumin' you can swim at all. Even if you can't, it's shallow here and you might almost be able to walk it. From that place to the mainland is but a short distance farther."

Becky approached and handed a small packet of food to Tyrone, who bowed with exaggerated courtesy. MacKenzie watched them with a grim smile on his lips.

"Y'd best tarry no longer now," he said. "For the alligators will be comin' out soon, to seek their evenin' meal!"

The morning sun was warm on their faces as John,

Becky and Jeremiah pushed off from the island to begin their long trek upstream and back cross-country to the city of St. Augustine.

It was a glorious Florida day. Not even a wisp of cloud appeared to mar the deep blue of the brilliant canopy overhead. The water about them shimmered with a million bright points of constantly moving light, and the air was soft and fresh. A bare hint of salt and seaweed spiced the gentle breeze at their backs.

When it came time for their nooning, John and Becky sat together talking quietly of many things. That evening, it was much the same.

Jeremiah was clearing pine cones away and digging a spot for his hips prior to spreading out his bedroll for the night when he paused and looked across the darkening clearing at MacKenzie.

"Been wonderin'," he said slowly, "just what you mean to do once we reach the settlements again. 'Case you've forgot, there's still a warrant out for your arrest and a considerable price on your head. I was thinkin' if you needed a man to stand by you here an' there — " he paused " — seein' that we're partners, like . . ."

John looked at the other man for a thoughtful moment before replying. "I'm grateful Jeremiah," he said at last, "and if there's ever the need you can be sure I'd call on you before any other. But I've hopes those matters can be settled without further occasion for trouble. Tyrone is out o' the picture now, and we've gold of our own to smooth the way."

He smiled. "And too, though I've been reluctant to ask the help o' those who've given me so much already, there are certain advantages to bein' the son of a prominent Carolina planter, the lifelong friend and associate o' such men as Governor James Grant and the brothers Moultrie!"

When the Negro had rolled in his blankets and closed his eyes, John looked down in the gathering twilight at the woman beside him.

"I've been thinkin'," he said, "o' somethin' you mentioned awhile back, on a bluff overlookin' another river. It seems to me that maybe after all a man might use a bit o' help with his plans, now an' again." He hesitated, suddenly embarrassed. "I mean, when it comes to raisin' tall, strong sons . . ."

Becky met his eyes boldly. "I'm glad you realize that, John MacKenzie, at the last." She turned then, taking his hand and gazing across the dark, slow-moving waters of the San Juanito.

"It's something we must discuss further — seeing that we're partners, like."

The End

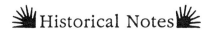Historical Notes

Alligator packs: Freshwater alligators, as well as their larger saltwater cousins, typically congregated in large groups of up to twenty or more until the species was decimated by hunters in the early 20th century. William Bartram, who visited Florida at about the same time as this story, offers a chilling account of one such pack in his *Travels*.

Battle between alligators and wild boars: The description in this novel is loosely adapted from a similar account in Cecile Hulse Matschat's *Suwannee River: Strange Green Land* (New York: Farrar & Rinehart Inc., 1938). Did it really happen? Matschat is ambivalent, presenting her version secondhand. But I am convinced that it *could* have happened. Few recent inhabitants of Florida are aware of the remarkable agility of the hunting alligator on land, to say nothing of the blind ferocity of the local wild boar or "piney woods rooter."

Black slaveholders: Think of it what one may, slavery

has been a worldwide practice from the beginnings of civilization until only a little over a century ago (and it is by no means extinct today). In most times and places it was not an issue of race, but of economic and social institutions. There was no law in Spanish or British Florida which prevented black freemen from keeping slaves as long as they had the means to purchase and support them; and some could and did. Many American Indians also held slaves — and had done so before Europeans or Africans ever set foot on these shores.

British Florida: At the Treaty of Paris in 1763, Florida was ceded to Britain by Spain as part of a complex transfer of territory following the Seven Years' War (known in this country as the French and Indian War). The area was divided into two colonies, West Florida (which extended to the Mississippi River) and East Florida with its capital at St. Augustine. The British ruled only until 1783, but during that twenty-year period they accomplished more in the way of development and colonization than the Spanish had in the past two hundred years. Many new residents stayed on under the subsequent Spanish rule, to become U. S. citizens with the final transfer of possession in 1821.

"Broad knife": For all intents and purposes, the knife carried by John MacKenzie is a Bowie knife. Such weapons were in use on the American frontier for years before Colonel Jim Bowie — who may or may not have made some small modifications — lent his name to them.

Buried treasure: As suggested in the story, this was a far less frequent occurrence than some of the more romantically-inclined would like to believe. There were plenty of places around the Caribbean where a pirate's haul could be readily exchanged for wine, women, etc. And for one whose hope of living to the age of thirty was slim at best, this made far more sense than "saving it for a rainy day." Besides, the risk of not finding the exact spot again after a few years of storms and shifting tides was far greater than many people imagine.

"Cabbage of the palm": The cabbage palm (*Sabal palmetto*) grows almost everywhere in the Florida peninsula, and the leaf-bud or "cabbage" at its top may be eaten either raw, cooked, or pickled. It has a pleasant nutty flavor, and is sometimes considered a delicacy. Unfortunately, removing this bud usually kills the tree — which is a more serious consideration today than it was in the sparsely populated Florida of the eighteenth century.

Flora, fauna, and general topography: Most of the locales described in this story are reasonably accurate, but the reader must understand that Florida is a very different country today than it was two hundred years ago — in great measure due to the persistent intrusion and immigration of *Homo sapiens*. The huge forests of cedar and virgin longleaf pine are now gone; the still abundant wildlife is but a trifle compared with the quantities of fish and game that once filled the land; and most modern residents can scarcely imagine flocks of birds so dense that they literally darkened the sky. Mother Nature has wrought her changes, too. Some ponds and lakes have dried up while others have formed; rivers have changed their courses; and no description of coastal lowlands from two centuries ago would be the same today, after the dozens of hurricanes and other storms which have ravaged the peninsula in the meantime.

Indenture: A custom of Colonial America by which individuals traded their personal liberty for passage to the New World. Not very different from slavery in fact, except that the indenture was initially voluntary, the period of servitude was limited (generally from 5 to 14 years), and those bound over were mainly Europeans. In the story, Tyrone is legally in the right. MacKenzie may be idealistic, but he is still abetting a criminal act by aiding Becky's escape.

The King's Road: A British improvement on existing routes between St. Augustine and Savannah. It crossed the St. Johns at the Cow Ford (present-day Jacksonville), continued north across the St. Marys near present-day Kings Ferry, Florida, and thence to Savannah. The road was later extended south to the New Smyrna settlement.

Natural bridge of the Santa Fe River: This is not what one usually thinks of as a "bridge" in the conventional sense, but rather a place where the river sinks into the earth and runs for some three miles underground before ree-merging near present-day High Springs. It does afford a way of crossing the Santa Fe without getting one's feet wet however, and thus was a well-known passage for travelers from pre-Columbian times well into the 19th century. It is now located within the boundaries of O'Leno State Park and Wildlife Preserve.

Old city wall: Much as described in this story. It extended from the fort (originally, and today, known as the Castillo de San Marcos) west to present-day Cordova Street in St. Augustine, then south along Maria Sanchez Creek to the vicinity of San Salvador Street, and east again to Matanzas

Inlet. Another wall ran westward across the narrow peninsula between the Fort and the San Sebastian River.

Patterns of speech: Modern readers may not always remember that all inhabitants of North America east of the Mississippi in 1773 were British subjects. Although there might be a few regional idiosyncrasies (especially on the frontier), their speech was not substantially different from the English of comparable social classes everywhere. Nor would one expect a Scotsman like MacKenzie, only a few generations removed from the old country and living largely in isolation with others of his kind, to have entirely lost his burr.

Pennsylvania rifle: Later known as the "Kentucky Rifle" (though frequently still manufactured by Pennsylvania gunsmiths), it was the most accurate firearm in the world for over a hundred years.

Posada: A Spanish inn. It has been reported that with the cession to Great Britain the Spanish left Florida "almost to a man." This was certainly true for the great majority of inhabitants — military or government officials and their dependents, who relied upon Spain for a living. But there were always exceptions. These would typically be "common folk," enterprising men and women who were capable of viewing change in terms of opportunity rather than loss.

San Juanito River: The early Spanish explorers believed that the St. Johns was part of a network of waterways which cut entirely across the Florida peninsula. When they found the mouth of another great river on the Gulf side, they naturally assumed it was a tributary of this system and called the second river Little St. Johns — San Juanito in Spanish. There are other theories to explain how the Suwannee River got its name, but if you say the two Spanish words quickly together the answer seems clear enough.

Sunbury: Town at the mouth of the Canoochee River, a few miles south of present-day Savannah. A major port of entry in Colonial times.

Trading posts in the wilderness: There have always been some rugged individualists who are inclined to set up business for themselves wherever they find a likely spot. The trader in this novel is such a man. It never occurred to him to wonder whether his post might eventually make it into maps or history books.

If you enjoyed reading this book, here are some other fiction titles from Pineapple Press. For a complete catalogue or to place an order, write to Pineapple Press, P.O. Drawer 16008, Southside Station, Sarasota, FL 34239, or call (800) PINEAPL.

Cracker Westerns:
Thunder on the St. Johns by Lee Gramling. Young Josh Carpenter and his family, homesteaders in 1850s Florida, join forces with an ex-gambler and a resourceful trapper's daughter to help settlers save their land from outlaws.

Guns of the Palmetto Plains by Rick Tonyan. As the Civil War explodes over Florida, Tree Hooker dodges Union soldiers and Florida outlaws to drive cattle to feed the starving Confederacy.

Riders of the Suwannee by Lee Gramling. Tate Barkley returns to 1870s Florida just in time to come to the aid of a young widow and her children as they fight to save their homestead from outlaws.

Other Florida Fiction:
Forever Island and *Allapattah* by Patrick Smith. *Forever Island* has been called the classic novel of the Everglades. *Allapattah* is the story of a young Seminole in despair in the white man's world.

The River is Home and *Angel City* by Patrick Smith. *The River is Home* tells of a Louisiana family's struggle to cope with changes in their rural environment. *Angel City* is a powerful and moving exposé of migrant workers in Florida in the 1970s.

A Land Remembered by Patrick Smith. Three generations of the MacIveys, a Florida family battling the hardships of the frontier to rise from a dirt-poor cracker life to the wealth and standing of real estate tycoons.